D1526093

FRENCH QUARTER CHRISTMAS

An Evil Dead MC Story

NICOLE JAMES

FRENCH QUARTER CHRISTMAS

An Evil Dead MC Story

By

Nicole James

PROLOGUE

Hope—

This client has been a regular with me for several years. Every time he comes to town, I make myself available. He's extremely wealthy and always treats me like a lady. Sometimes I accompany him to a show, like the one we saw tonight, and then return to the hotel for a private dinner.

"Tim McGraw was phenomenal. Thank you for taking me." I took a sip of my wine.

"Thank you for accompanying me. As always, I was the envy of every man in the room."

"You are too sweet."

We sat at a candlelit table. He reached for the bottle of wine and refilled my glass. His phone went off, and he put it to his ear, stepping away to take the call.

He finished and returned, taking my hand and pulling me to my feet.

"Is everything all right?" I frowned.

He held my chin and dropped a kiss to my lips.

"I have to leave, beautiful. Something's come up in New York. It's urgent. The penthouse is paid through Friday. Stay. Use the spa. Have a massage. Get a pedicure. Whatever you'd like. Charge it to the room. Enjoy yourself."

"Are you sure?"

"Yes. I'll see you again soon. Next month, perhaps."

I was always available to Mr. Black, even if it was last minute. I made myself available at the drop of a hat for this man. He was one of my easiest and best customers.

"Until then, Hope."

Hope Hill. That was me. One of the most expensive escorts on the Strip. I didn't have sex with my customers. I didn't have to. What they got with me was an unattainable woman on their arm. The ones I saw wanted company to bring to an event or such.

I knew my beauty was rare, so I used it to my advantage. I gave my clients a lovely time, good conversation, and I hung on their every word. They all came back for more. They knew the score. No sex. It didn't matter. I was still in high demand. I was smart enough to know my value, therefore I didn't come cheap. My looks wouldn't last forever, so I had to make the most of them while I could. This wasn't my dream job. That was what I was saving up for. I had plans. Someday I'd achieve them.

Mr. Black slipped into his suit jacket, gathered his toiletry bag, and disappeared through the door.

Then I was alone in the four-thousand dollar a night penthouse—mine to use for two more nights.

***

Lobo—

I walked out of the Las Vegas Municipal Courthouse into the Thursday afternoon sun and loosened my tie. I never wore suits and had to buy this one for the occasion. "Wear a suit," my lawyer had said. "It's important," he'd underscored. I'd even shaved my damn beard for this.

Did it make a damn bit of difference? No.

Did we win our case? Fuck no.

"Come on. Let's get a drink."

My eyes shifted to my neighbor. He was a young internist at the local hospital, barely out of medical school and already going through his first divorce.

He'd been suckered by the same real estate developer as me. Braddock Homes. They'd promised a nice neighborhood complete with sidewalks and a community pool with clubhouse. I was sucker enough to sign on for one of the first builds. So was Tom.

What we and the other two plaintiffs in our class-action lawsuit ended up with was four houses at the end of a cul-de-sac in the middle of barren land. No sidewalks, no pool or clubhouse, no subdivision.

Now we were all stuck there until another builder bought out the tanked business and finished it. Our lawyer told us it could take years. Until then, our property value was in the toilet, making it impossible to sell and come out on top. We were all now underwater on our home values.

I should have listened to Daytona. He told me not to jump the gun, but no, I was so fucking sure this house was going to be a promise of a new future, one with a wife and kids. I wanted those things before I was too old to get them.

Last thing I wanted was to become some aged biker with nothing but high school dropout club girls to choose from. I thought Candy had been my future. Turns out being tied down wasn't her idea of fun. She'd led me down that path, then suddenly got cold feet. Unfortunately, it had been after I'd signed on the dotted line.

Now I was fucked.

I climbed into Tom's car. He was about five years younger, but it seemed like a much bigger gap. He was into the club scene and picking up hot tourists. That's what had gotten him into trouble with his wife and spelled the end of his marriage. He'd picked up some hot babe in town for a bachelorette party. He was an idiot. But right now, he was my ride.

It was a twenty-minute drive from downtown to the Strip. The place was crowded with tourists.

"I'm not interested in going to a club," I said, looking at the masses working their way down the busy sidewalks.

"I know the perfect place."

We passed Caesar's Palace and the Bellagio until Tom finally turned into an entrance.

"This used to be the Mandarin Oriental Hotel before it was bought out."

I took his word for it, not really caring.

He pulled under the crystal portico, and a valet hurried forward to take his car.

We walked inside. The place was grander than anything I'd seen. The Strip with its fancy hotels wasn't my cup of tea. I rode a Harley. I was a member of an MC, though I'm not sure my neighbor knew that. If it wasn't for this lawsuit, I doubt we'd even be having this drink together.

I straightened my tie and followed him to the elevator.

He hit the button for the 23rd floor, and it whisked us skyward.

"Most people don't know this bar is here, because it occupies a cool little corner of the 23rd floor. Locals call it the Corner Bar."

"If no one knows about it, who goes here?"

"A well-heeled crowd of mostly guests who definitely care what they're drinking, but more importantly, care about being taken care of."

"So, a bunch of snooty rich people. Great."

Tom chuckled as the doors opened. "Come on, don't you want to see how the other half lives?"

"Not really." But I followed him inside. The place had two floor-to-ceiling glass walls that met in the corner. I found myself looking out over an amazing view of the Strip. The bar was sophisticated and slick—a vibe I'm sure this place had perfected throughout the hotel.

I liked that it was quiet enough I could actually hear a conversation, and it wasn't a dance club. No giggling bachelorette parties in sight. Thank God.

We grabbed a seat at the bar. The wall behind it held glass shelves with liquor bottles in a nice backlit amber lighting.

A bartender took our order, and I glanced around. The place wasn't too busy, with only a handful of guests. It was early yet, and the sun was going down, splashing the distant mountains in golden color. One of my favorite times of day.

"So now what? Do we try to sue Braddock's insurance company for the money?" I asked, taking a sip of my bourbon. I wasn't sure I had the money for more legal fees.

"That or go to arbitration or mediation."

"Sounds like a lose-lose. What I'd like to do is find the owner of Braddock Homes and beat the shit out of him."

It wasn't long before Tom left me to talk up two blondes at a table by the windows. I'm sure the first words out of his mouth were he was an ER doctor specializing in neurology.

Dick.

I studied the reflection behind the bar, and my eyes locked on a woman near the end. She was beautiful—stunning, really—with long, thick honey blonde hair. She was in a sexy, elegant black dress. It and the clutch on the bar top spoke money. Her hemline was short, and my gaze traveled over the length of her leg to her stilettos.

She sipped on what looked like a lemon drop martini, its sugared rim and twist of lemon giving it away. Her nails were long and red, and I suddenly had an image of them lightly scratching the inked skin of my chest.

My dick liked the image and jumped to attention.

Down, boy.

A man one stool over shifted to the one next to the beauty at the bar and leaned in, talking in her ear. She pulled back, and I almost smiled, wondering if he had bad breath.

She tried to maintain her cool, and though I couldn't hear what she was saying, I knew she was trying to be gracious, but dismissive.

This guy wasn't taking the hint.

His big hand landed on her thigh and gave a squeeze. She grabbed his wrist and pushed it off. The man went right back for more.

I hated men who thought they could take whatever they wanted. I'd seen too much of it in my life. If the bartender had noticed, I'm sure security would have been on the scene in moments and escorted him away. But this girl didn't look like she wanted trouble or attention. There was something in her face that made me think she thought she somehow deserved this. She looked almost beaten down. Whatever it was, it had me downing my drink, standing from my stool, and approaching. I slid onto the seat on her other side.

"I hope I didn't keep you waiting too long, darling. The traffic was horrendous. What a way to start our night on the town for our anniversary, huh? How was your day?"

The woman looked up, confusion in her eyes at first. Her gaze swept down my suit.

"I knew you wouldn't miss our anniversary, dear."

The man on her other side pulled back. "I thought you were alone."

I straightened as if I'd just noticed the guy. "What's this? You bothering my wife, buddy?"

At six-three, I stood over the short, balding man. His eyes widened, and he lifted his palms with his sausage fingers and his pinkie ring. "Oh, sorry. Didn't know she was your wife."

"Take off," I grunted, giving him the same look that had backed down many an asshole.

"Sure. Sure. I don't want any trouble."

"Trouble's what you'll get if you don't get the fuck out of here."

His face flamed red, and he stalked out.

The bartender came over. "Is there a problem, ma'am?"

She sipped her drink, but I noticed her hand trembled. "No. Thank you. Everything's fine."

I slipped back onto the stool. "Sorry. I saw him pawing at you. It didn't look like you wanted his attention. I hope I wasn't out of line."

"Not at all. I appreciate it. Thank you."

"You're welcome." I studied her face. "Mind if I stay?"

"Please do."

"I bet you get that often." I nodded to the door.

"Men hitting on me?"

"Men thinking they can take what they want," I corrected.

"Not usually in a place as nice as this, but yes, it happens."

She set her glass down and ran her finger along the stem. She looked sad.

"You okay?"

She nodded.

She obviously didn't want to talk about it, so I tried to change the subject. I glanced around. "I've never been in here before, have you?"

"Many times."

That had my head swiveling. "Really?"

"On business."

"I see."

"I doubt you do, but that's okay. What do you do for a living?"

I tilted my head, not really wanting to do what always felt to me like an interview. "How about we dispense with the usual getting to know you chit-chat? What I do, what you do? Blah, blah, blah. Let's not play that game."

"Then what would that leave us to talk about?"

"More interesting things. No names or occupations or how long you've been in town. Let's keep the mystery. Nothing personal."

"Sounds good to me." She lifted her chin. "With one exception."

"What's that?"

"You're not married, are you?"

"Nope. You?"

"No."

"Good. Let's be different people. I'll be a pilot for the airlines. Who do you want to be? Pick something exciting."

She smiled at the game, relaxing a bit. "I've always wanted to be an FBI agent."

I chuckled. "Are you into handcuffs?"

She winked. "I could be."

I nodded to her glass. "Need another, Agent Hotcakes?"

She almost spit out her drink but didn't miss a beat with her comeback. "I'd love one, Captain Longcock."

"Damn near on the mark, angel."

"That remains to be seen, darling."

"Well, it is our anniversary, right?"

"It is. I'd forgotten."

"Maybe you'll get lucky."

"Indeed. I do have the key to a room."

I arched a brow. "Do you now? Hmm. Things could get interesting."

"You play your cards right, Captain, and they just might."

I motioned the bartender over. "The lady needs a refill, and I'll have a Jameson on the rocks."

When he brought them, I raised my glass. "Here's to making you smile, beautiful."

"You seem like a fun guy."

"I am. Lots of fun." I slipped my phone from my pocket and wrapped an arm around her. "Let's get a picture. Smile."

Two drinks later, she led me to the elevators. I studied our reflection in the smoked mirrored glass. We looked good together. She was stunning—the kind of woman I never thought was in my league. But I was wearing a suit, and somehow that wasn't really me. This was a dream, a fantasy. It couldn't be real, and yet it was.

The doors opened, and we stepped on.

She hit the button for the penthouse floor. That threw me, but I didn't say anything. My eyes dropped to her lips, and I wanted to press her up against the elevator wall and kiss her, but I knew she deserved better than to be mauled in an elevator. Perhaps I was wrong. Maybe that was exactly what she wanted. I'd met a lot of women who craved a walk on the wild side. They'd see the leather, the Harley, the tattoos, and the bad boy fantasy would kick in.

Tonight, I was none of those things. She had no clue that was who she was getting. In a way, it was freeing. Yeah, those things could feel like armor; I put on that vest, and I became that guy. Without it, I was free to be someone else. Someone different.

The ding sounded, and the doors slid open. There appeared to be four penthouses on this floor. She led me to the door on the right. When it swung open, I was greeted with more opulence than I'd ever seen. It was a palatial apartment with exquisite furnishings. The view alone was stunning, and I could only imagine this place ran into the thousands per night.

I turned to her.

She smiled when she saw the look on my face. "You weren't ready for this, were you?"

"No, ma'am. I'm a little shocked, actually. You rich?"

"I'm an FBI Agent, remember?" She winked, and I chuckled.

"Right." I got the hint. No names, no questions, nothing real. That was the deal.

Suddenly, she looked a little nervous. Like now that she had me here, she didn't know what to do with me.

That was okay. I was fine taking the lead. I reached for her hand. "Give me a tour."

That seemed to put her at ease as we walked from the entryway farther into the suite. A living room faced a corner of glass windows that looked out over the lights of the Strip. It was truly spectacular.

A tablet was mounted to the wall. I tugged on her hand. "Can this thing play music?"

"I suppose so." She used the touch screen to scroll through the menu. "What do you like?"

"Something mellow and bluesy."

She found a smooth blues channel, and the room filled with the sounds.

She led me through a hall. We passed an enormous bathroom with a standalone tub in front of floor-to-ceiling windows. It looked big enough for two, and immediately I was making plans to make use of it later.

The next stop on the tour was the bedroom. It, too, was a corner room with impressive floor-to-ceiling windows. The bed was a king with plenty of pillows and expensive bedding.

There was a certain nervousness in her eyes. She looked vulnerable, fragile, and it made me want to hold her, to treat her gently.

I tilted her chin with the side of my curled finger, brushing the soft skin with my thumb, and stared into those liquid dark eyes. She had that sexy smoky-eye thing going that girls did with their makeup, and she was damn good at it. I could have drowned in those dark pools.

Her lips were plump and pink.

I wanted to kiss her and lay her out on that giant bed and worship her body, but I needed to put her at ease first.

"There's nothing to worry about, angel. If you need this slow and easy, I'll give you that. If you want to stop, just say the word, and I'll leave."

"I don't want you to leave," she whispered.

"Good." I kissed her, my tongue exploring, coaxing hers, until she was coming back for more every time I retreated.

Her hands moved to my chest and slipped under my suit coat, pushing it off my shoulders to fall to the floor. If it had been my cut, I wouldn't have liked that. My colors never touch the floor. Club rules. But I didn't give a damn about the suit jacket.

Her hands moved to my tie, tugging and loosening it, then slipping it free and tossing it aside. She lifted one of my wrists and worked the cuff free. I studied her as she did and dipped my head to nuzzle her temple and breathe in her scent.

"What's the name of your perfume?"

She glanced up as she worked the other cuff free. "Bombshell."

I threaded my fingers through her honey curls. "Bombshell. It suits you."

I pulled her to me and kissed her again while her fingers worked the buttons down my chest free. I shrugged out of the shirt, revealing my skin. It was dim in the room with just the lights from the Strip— the world's best nightlight. She studied my tattoos, but I don't think she could tell exactly what they were. With my club, skulls had a significant symbolism. Mine were colorful, and the art was primo stuff I'd paid a mint for.

If she was surprised, she covered it well.

I spun her around and found the fastening for her dress, undoing it and letting it fall to the floor.

She turned to me in a sexy black lace bra and panty set, the kind that didn't come cheap. I ran a finger under one strap. "I like this."

"Do you?"

"Yeah. Take it off."

She smiled and slipped the bra off first, and her breasts popped forth, full and gorgeous.

I whistled. "You are gorgeous, Agent Hot Cakes.

That got a giggle out of her.

"Lay on the bed."

She did as I asked. Kneeling, I slipped her heels off, then ran my palms along the silky skin of her legs, up her shapely calves to her thighs. I pressed a kiss to her knee and made a trail of them up the inside of her thigh, my destination clearly that lace-covered pussy.

Pressing a kiss over the fabric, I bit the edge between my teeth and dragged it down her thighs.

Her belly quivered as she writhed and lifted her hips. I tossed the panties on the carpet near my jacket, fully intending to keep them as a memento.

She lay before me, naked.

I reached for my belt buckle. Her eyes dropped, following my motions as I worked it open and undid my slacks.

She licked her lips, and I felt my already hard dick jump.

The need to take her surged through me, my heart pounding and my blood rushing through my veins, but I had to keep myself in check. I wanted to savor every moment with this woman.

Pulling a short strip of condoms from my wallet, I tossed them on the bed next to her. Her head twisted to look.

"Three, hmm? Aren't you ambitious?"

I grinned. "Yes, ma'am."

I got naked, and her gaze roamed over me. My cock stood long and hard. I grasped the thick shaft in my hand and stroked it, root to crown.

Her chest rose and fell, and she bit her bottom lip. The image of that mouth wrapped around my dick filled my head. We'd get there, I hoped, but there were things I wanted to do first, and I knew the minute she sucked me inside that pretty mouth, it'd be a race to the finish.

I dropped to my knees at the foot of the bed, grabbed her ankles, and dragged her to the end of the bed. She gasped as she slid along the comforter, but the way her eyes flared told me she liked being manhandled, liked me taking control. I put her legs over my shoulders, moving in, and then stroked my thumbs over her pussy. She jumped at the first touch.

"Shh, baby girl. I'll be gentle. There's no rush." I stroked her again, slow and easy. She was wet, and I needed a taste. I dipped my head. The first swipe of the flat of my tongue had her shuddering and moaning. I went back for more, again and again, until she was lifting to meet my mouth.

My tongue tunneled inside her wet channel and then up to seek and circle her clit. She jumped again, then bucked against me. I grasped the back of her knees and pinned her to the bed. Then I took my sweet time, spending eons on the sensitive bud that peeked out until her hands were fisting handfuls of comforter. I released one leg and slipped two fingers into that sweet, tight pussy.

"Fuck, yes, baby girl." I stroked with my fingertips, searching out that secret spot deep inside her, while my thumb drew circles around her clit.

Glancing up, I found her watching me, her eyes liquid, her teeth in her lower lip. Her breasts jiggled as she moved, reminding me I hadn't even gotten to those beauties yet. I found the spot I was looking for, and her back arched, her mouth dropping open. I shifted, moving over her, and while I kept at her with my fingers and thumb, never letting up, I captured one tight hard nipple in my mouth. I toyed with it, nibbled at it, and sucked hard.

She bucked against my hand. Pleading. "Don't stop."

Her breathing increased, her chest heaving, and I moved from one breast to the other, never letting up my strokes. Finally, she bucked and moaned, collapsing as my fingers felt a new rush of wetness coating them.

I slowly withdrew as she moaned again, then I carried my wet fingers to her mouth. I painted her lips.

"Open."

She did as I told her, and I slipped my two fingers inside that sweet mouth. She sucked them clean, then I pulled them free and kissed her, tasting her on my tongue again. She wriggled beneath me, and I knew I couldn't wait much longer to have her, but she had different ideas, pushing me to my back and sliding down the bed. I moved to the headboard, leaning against it as she moved between my legs and grasped my hard-as-a-rock dick in her hand and guided it to her waiting mouth. She gave it a long lick, then ran the head of it around her lips before taking it to the back of her throat in one movement.

I sucked in a breath. "Christ, that's good." I cupped her head, brushing her hair back and loving the sight of my wet cock sliding in and out of her lips. "That's a gorgeous sight."

I rolled my hips, matching her movements and urging her on. When I was about to come, I rolled us until she was on her back, then I moved to my knees, tore open the condom wrapper with my teeth, and rolled it on.

With my dick in my hand, I guided it to her pussy, then circled the head around the rim of her entrance and coated it until it was slick.

"You want me, baby?" I asked.

"Yes. Please. Take me."

I slid inside her in one hard thrust, all the way to the hilt. I stilled and enjoyed the feeling of her tight pussy clenching around me. Staring into her eyes, I wanted to commit this moment to my memory. My palm cupped her face. I felt a connection with this woman, this stranger I didn't know existed a few hours ago.

It felt like everything had changed somehow. Like my life had just been marked in two equal parts. All the days before her, and every day from this point on. It was the weirdest feeling. I tried to brush it aside and concentrate on fucking this gorgeous gift from God.

I rocked against her, rubbing over her clit and dragging the shaft of my cock along it with every thrust.

Soon she was panting again, thrashing on the bed. I kept the pace, building her orgasm stroke by stroke, until she was desperate for me to go faster.

"Please, baby. Fuck me harder."

I gave her what she wanted, and I knew I wasn't going to be able to last much longer. I'd been damn near ready to blow since the moment I slid inside her perfect pussy.

"Touch me," I ordered, and her hands stroked up my chest to cup my neck and pull me down for a kiss. I did a pushup, bringing my mouth to hers.

I was breathing too hard to hold it for long and broke off, pressing my forehead to hers, the air surging in and out of my lungs.

"Fuck, you're gorgeous, lady. Such a tight, wet pussy you have."

Her breasts bounced with every slam of my hips, and I couldn't drag my eyes from them. I dipped my head and sucked one, then the other. I came hard, going rock solid against her as she screamed out her own ecstasy. I collapsed on top of her, breathing hard.

Her soft hands stroked over my back. I roused enough to press a kiss to her cleavage, then lifted off her.

She tried to grab at me. "Don't go."

"Just need to deal with the condom."

"Hurry back."

While I was in the bathroom, my eyes fell on that tub again. I walked over and ran the water, adjusting it to the perfect temperature. It was filling quickly, so I returned to the bed and scooped my beautiful girl into my arms.

She held onto my neck and laid her head on my shoulder. I pressed a kiss to her head. I'd left the lights off, so we only had the lights of the Strip. It was almost as good as candlelight. I set her in the steaming water and joined her, cuddling her between my legs with her back to my chest. Then I reached for the expensive soap and poured some in my hand. I washed every inch of her as a bluesy melody played in the background.

She leaned her head on my shoulder. "Mmm. This is exquisite."

I dribbled water over her breasts, watching the rivulets run down to her nipples where they dripped to the water.

"I wish I had my phone so I could snap a picture of you."

"No nude pictures."

"Yes, ma'am." I licked her neck. "Guess I'll just have to rely on my memory."

We lingered in the bath a long time and stared at the view of the city that never sleeps. I stroked my fingers over her taught nipples. I couldn't seem to keep my hands off her breasts.

Her head lolled on my shoulder, and she moaned when I detoured my fingers between her legs.

"Tell me something real," I whispered in her ear, then bit the lobe.

She rolled her head and stared out the window. I was afraid I'd ruined things, thinking I should have kept to the rules, but she whispered an answer.

"I've never felt this way with a man. Ever. Is that real enough for you?"

"I feel the same. Like every day I've walked on this planet before I met you meant nothing."

She twisted in my arms and met my eyes, as if she was judging the truth of my words.

"I mean it. Every word."

She swallowed and dropped her eyes, shifting back.

"What? Does that make you nervous or something?"

She shook her head.

"What is it? Tell me?"

"This was just supposed to be fun, but somehow it feels more serious than any conversation I've ever had. Do you believe in things like fate?"

I stroked her shoulder, running the tips of my fingers along her skin. "Not before tonight. Now? Maybe. I wasn't supposed to be here. In that hotel bar. I don't usually frequent places like that. I'm not a guest of this hotel. It was such a random thing. I'd caught a ride with an acquaintance back from a meeting we had earlier. This isn't my world. What are the odds you and I would ever meet?"

"Astronomical," she murmured.

"I know we said no questions, but I have to ask. What are you doing here, in this city, in this penthouse suite? Where did you come from? Now I want to know everything."

"We let our guard down for the very reason we didn't let any of that get in the way. Don't ruin it. Please."

The water was turning cool, and I felt like she didn't want to talk anymore. "You ready to dry off?"

She nodded in a sad way, and it was like things had changed. I hated that.

I pushed my hands on the rim and hoisted myself up, then held her hand and helped her step out. Grabbing a thick, plush towel, I dried her off, taking my time.

She did the same for me, her eyes traveling over every inch of me as she did. I wondered what she thought of the ink, but she never asked. She was a rule follower; I was the rule breaker. Hell, I'd broken more rules in my life than I could count. How could a man like me ever deserve a woman like her?

I'd been blessed for even one night.

Scooping her in my arms, I carried her back to the bed.

We used the remaining condoms before dropping into an exhausted sleep. It felt good wrapped around her, my leg thrown over hers, her ass cuddled against my perpetually hard dick. Her curvy body fit perfectly in my arms. It felt right.

I closed my eyes and drifted off.

***

The morning sun streaming in the windows woke me. I cracked an eye and squinted into the light, moaning and rolling over, my arm extended across the cool sheets. But my palm came up empty. She was gone.

I sat up, looking toward the bathroom. "Babe?"

No answer. The room was dead quiet.

I slipped from the bed and yanked on my boxer briefs and slacks and searched the place. Nothing. I looked for her shoes, her clutch, her luggage. Nothing.

Backtracking to the bed, I found a note on the nightstand written on hotel stationary. I picked it up.

Captain LC—
It was glorious.
XO—
Agent HC
P.S. Check out is at 11am

I carried it to my nose and breathed in the scent of her perfume. She'd sprayed it on the note, evidently.

Like a glass slipper, it was all I had left of her.

CHAPTER ONE

Lobo—

Standing in my kitchen, peering in the fridge, one hand on the door, I stared at the mostly empty shelves and scratched my stomach. Christ, I needed to shop, but I avoided the grocery store like the plague. Nothing I hated more than pushing those dumb carts around with their squeaky, wobbly wheels. I glanced over the top of the door at my club president and VP. "How about Taco Shack, prez?"

"Tacos? I thought you had brats you were gonna grill for us? It's finally cool enough to actually grill outside."

"Sorry. Guess I'm out."

Trick chuckled. "You forget you didn't have any food in the house, or are you losing your mind?"

"All of the above, maybe. Get off my back, VP."

He let it drop for the time being, and his eyes hit my stack of mail on the counter. The invitation sticking out of its engraved envelope caught his attention and he picked it up, his eyes scanning the scrolling words. "What's this?"

Damn, I should have stashed it in a drawer. "Invitation to a Christmas party."

"Oh, really?" My president straightened in his chair at my kitchen table. "Toss it here."

Trick complied, and Daytona caught it in midair, flipping the envelope over. "Jacqueline Broussard," he read. "Who's that?"

"My grandmother."

"That your last name? Broussard?"

"Yep."

"Never knew that."

"There's a lot of shit you don't know, prez." I smirked.

"Smartass." He continued reading. "New Orleans, huh? That home?"

"Yep."

Trick reached past me and grabbed a longneck off the top shelf. "You're just full of secrets, aren't you? I thought you were from California."

"New Orleans was a long time ago."

He moved to the table and plopped in a chair next to Daytona. "So, you goin' home for Christmas this year, then?"

"Nope." I grabbed a bottle for myself and one for prez and shut the fridge, giving up on lunch.

Daytona snagged the beer I held out and met my eyes. "No? I thought you told me a while back your grandmother was sick."

"She is." I dropped into a chair across from him, wishing I'd kept my mouth shut.

"So, you don't feel a need to spend this Christmas with her? What if it's her last?"

I shrugged, twisted the cap off my bottle and downed a good portion, feeling the cold liquid on the back of my throat. I didn't want to think about this being her last, or that soon I might lose her.

Daytona dropped the envelope and opened his own bottle, leaning in his chair. "Don't give me that bullshit. I know you better than that."

"I went ten years ago." The excuse sounded lame, even in my ears.

Daytona huffed out a laugh. "Ten years. Well then, no one could expect more from you than that."

His words cut. "Don't be a wiseass."

He set his bottle on the table and lit a cigarette. "What's the problem? Why don't you want to go home?"

I shrugged, wondering why he gave a damn. "My grandmother expects things out of me, okay? I don't want to disappoint her."

Daytona blew smoke toward the ceiling. "What things?"

"Man, you're full of questions today."

"Just tell me."

"She's wanted me married with kids for years now. I promised her next time she saw me, I'd have a start on that. I hate to see the look in her eyes when I come home alone again. I'd rather avoid the whole thing."

Trick chuckled. "You, a disappointment? No way."

I rolled my eyes.

Daytona studied me. "That's a load of crap, Lobo, and it's a shitty reason for not going to see her."

"Whatever."

Trick put in his two cents. "Take one of the club girls. Surely one of them can pretend to be your girlfriend. They'd only have to do it for a day or two."

"That's not the kind of chick my gran wants to see me with, and you know it."

"How about Trix?" Daytona suggested.

"With all her ink? No way."

He cocked a brow. "So, you're open to the idea. Now we need to nail down the right candidate for the job."

"And what? Be my fake fiancée? Pretend we're in a relationship? Listen to yourself. The idea is crazy."

Trick shook his head. "It's not. It's a win-win for you and Grandma. She dies a happy woman, and you get to go home again. To tell the truth, brother, I think it'd do you some good. You haven't been yourself lately."

"What the fuck's that supposed to mean?"

He jabbed a finger at me. "Right there. That's what I'm talking about. You're edgy all the time and take offense to every damn thing."

"I do not."

"Quit," Daytona snapped, then focused on me. "Look, I know things have been a little hard to deal with since that disaster with Candy last year."

"I do not want to talk about that bitch."

"All I'm sayin' is, lesson learned, right? Time to shake that shit off and move on."

"I've moved on."

"Moving on and letting go is not your strong suit, brother. You hang on to shit for years."

"Ain't that the truth," Trick added.

"What the fuck's with both of you? Is this gang up on Lobo day?" They both needed to drop it. Especially since Prez didn't know how close to the truth about why I didn't want to go home he actually was.

"Look, all I'm sayin' is, maybe it's time to reconnect with family. Get around someone besides the club. Someone who knew you from a child. Someone who knows all your secrets."

"Secrets are best left alone, prez."

"Yeah. You're the king of secrets, all right. You keep everything locked up tight. You need to relax and let the tough-guy image go for a few days. Go home. Unwind for the holidays. It'll do you good. That's an order."

"Only place I'm goin' is to the garage to work on my bike. Feel free to drink all my beer." I shoved to my feet and stalked out, slamming the door behind me. I was good with ribbing. Everyone in the club did it all the time, but this hit too close to home and touched on the guilt I'd been carrying around since the moment that invitation arrived. Gran and I had always had a special relationship, and I hadn't seen her in years. What if this was her last Christmas? If I didn't go home, would that be another thing I'd regret for the rest of my life?

***

Daytona—

I looked over at my VP. "You know anybody he can take home for Christmas?"

Trick almost spit his beer out. "You mean play his fake girlfriend? Hell no. Unless you want me to talk to one of the girls at the house."

The house being the place we housed the girls we'd hired to do internet porn. I didn't want to fuck up those business relationships with having any of them involved with the boys in the club. I shook my head, something in the back of my mind pulling at me. When it came to me, I snapped my fingers. "Wasn't there some girl he talked about right after he broke up with Candy?"

Trick straightened and laughed. "You mean that chick who ran out on him? The one he went on about for days?"

"Yeah, her."

"Boss, how am I supposed to find her?"

"Thought you knew everyone in town?"

"Vegas is a big place."

"He had a picture of the two of them at a bar. Didn't you say you thought she looked familiar?"

"She looked like Hope Hill, but that would have been impossible. She's the most expensive escort on the Strip. She'd hardly go slumming with our Sgt at Arms."

"He wasn't wearin' his cut that night. He said he never told her who he was."

Trick shrugged like it didn't care.

"Okay, whatever. Maybe it's not her, but that gives me an idea. Let's hire this girl. This Hope Hill."

"Did you not hear the part when I said she's the most expensive escort on the Strip? You payin' for this? She's gonna cost a mint. Especially if it involves multiple days and flying to New Orleans."

"Can you get in touch with her or not?"

"I'm sure the concierge at the Regency can give me a number for the right price."

"Find out what this will cost me."

"Why the hell do you care so much if Lobo goes home for Christmas?"

"Look at this place. Does this say home to you?"

"It's a nice house."

"He got it because he thought things were going somewhere with Candy. It's obvious he wants more out of life than just the club. And you're right, it's a nice house, but it's not a home, Trick. It's not what I have with Cherry, and it's not what you have with Anna."

He glanced around at the sparsely furnished rooms. "So, it's minimalist. Maybe he likes that."

"Hogwash. It's not just the décor. The man comes home to an empty house every night—a house where he thought he was going to start a family."

"You don't know he comes home alone. For all we know, he may have a different woman in here every night."

"Like who? You heard of anybody? No, you haven't. None of us have. The man is lonely, and he obviously wants something more than what the club girls have to offer him."

"So how is paying for an escort gonna help him?"

"Something needs to shake him up. I think this trip home is just the ticket. But the only way he's goin' is if he's got a woman in tow.

Maybe he'll find what he's looking for in New Orleans. I got a feeling he's got unresolved issues. You and I both know those can eat a man from the inside out."

"Guess so." Trick shrugged. "Not sure I agree this is the solution, but if this is the way you want to play this, I'll make some calls and get you a figure."

I slapped his shoulder. "Don't worry. I'll get you a nice Christmas present, too."

"No hookers. Anna would kill me."

"You said she was a high-end escort, not a hooker."

"Right. Not sure there's a difference."

"There's a difference. Bet she'll clarify it for you when you talk to her."

"Guess so." He scrolled through his phone.

I picked up my beer, smiling, suddenly feeling like fucking Santa Claus.

CHAPTER TWO

Hope—

I knocked on the front door of the ranch-style house and glanced around the neighborhood, if you could call it that. Four houses on the end of a cul-de-sac, like a development that was abandoned before it got past the four model homes. It sat on the edge of town, where the desert opened into rugged beauty with the Spring Mountains in the distance.

This was farther than I'd ever come for a job. Usually, I did not need to leave the Strip. But I needed the money, and this guy was willing to pay—or should I say, his boss was. The whole circumstances of this client and job were a little hazy, and that made me nervous.

I usually stuck with previous clients or clients who found me through acquaintances. I did a lot of conventions and business trips, acting as their companion or date. I rarely did overnights or traveled.

This was against most of my rules.

If the man paying hadn't been a personal friend of Mickey's—the concierge at the Regency—and if I didn't need the money, I would have turned it down.

My hand tightened around my fake Louis Vuitton travel bag. I couldn't afford the real thing, but I need to look the part. Most of my clients were wealthy and traveled in circles where certain expectations of attire ruled.

It was important I always looked chic and pulled together, and I used a small portion of my earnings for clothing and accessories and banked the rest. If I ever wanted to escape this life and fulfill my dream, I had to save as much as I could. I was getting so close. That's why I agreed to take this job. The bonus offered was too much to turn down.

I knocked again, then pushed the doorbell.

A man yanked the door open, and I stared at a bare chest I recognized. My mouth dropped open, and I pulled my sunglasses off.

My shock was reflected in his eyes.

"God, I never thought I'd see you again." His gaze swept over me, taking in my cream linen walking shorts and matching vest that revealed my bare arms and a good portion of leg to my high heels. I'd topped off the outfit with a wide-brimmed sunhat and a chunky strand of braided pearls. "How did you find me?"

I took a step back. "I'm not sure I'm at the right house."

"What are you doing in Vegas?" And then his face changed as it dawned on him. He let out a frustrated sigh and lifted a brow. "Christ, you're the one they hired? You're an *escort?*"

Oh, crap. *He's* my client? The man I snuck out on, too afraid of my reaction to him to stick around and find out where it went. The man who'd rocked my world in that fabulous penthouse. I just stared, wondering how to extricate myself from this situation. I turned. "I'm sorry. I had no idea…"

He opened the door wider before I could escape. "Come in."

I swallowed and rolled my carry-on inside, not knowing what else to do.

He extended his hand. "They call me Lobo."

"I'm Hope. Hope Hill."

"Nice to meet you, Hope. Our flight leaves soon, so I've got to hurry." He moved toward the kitchen and pulled a dress shirt off the back of a chair, slipping it on and doing up the cuffs. I stared at his chest some more before it disappeared behind the buttons. "So, this is what you do for a living?"

It sounded like an accusation, so I didn't give him an answer. My eyes slid to the leather vest hanging on another chair. *Evil Dead MC, Nevada.* My eyes widened. "You're a biker?"

He followed my gaze. "They didn't tell you?"

I cleared my throat. "No, they did not."

"Does it matter?"

"Maybe." It was like Dr. Jekyll and Mr. Hyde. Had I just met Mr. Hyde? I knew next to nothing about this man, yet I felt like I knew everything. Had that all been fake? The way he was with me had been tender, gentle. Was that the kind of man he truly was? That black leather vest hanging six feet away said otherwise. What had I gotten myself into?

Evidently, he read the panic in my eyes.

"Look, I need someone to pretend to be my girlfriend over Christmas. No strings. I don't expect anything. Just some acting the part when we're in front of family. Think you can do that?"

I straightened. "That's all this is, then? A job? You didn't know…"

"How was I supposed to know? You think I tracked you down and hired you?"

My hand hit my hip. "Well, you seemed to think *I* tracked *you* down."

"You show up at my door out of the blue. What was I supposed to believe? This is all just a big coincidence?"

"Evidently. Did you think I'd ever want you to know what I did?"

"Obviously not. Well, you're here now. So, how 'bout it? Think you can do the job and be my fake girlfriend for the weekend?"

I sighed. That was the question at hand. Could he be a job to me after what we'd shared? I'd already taken the money. I'd paid bills. It was long gone. I had no choice but to carry through, so I straightened my shoulders. "Of course."

"Good. Then career choices shouldn't matter, should they?" His gaze perused me again, like I was somehow less in his eyes now that he knew what I did. I wonder if the way I'd looked at that biker vest of his conveyed the same judgment.

"Not at all," I bit out.

"Though, I gotta say, I don't like liars."

"Me neither." I arched a brow. I could give back as good as I got.

He slipped a suit coat on and tugged at the cuffs, adjusting the shirt below. It was amazing how the outfit changed the man. He looked civilized, like he had the night we'd met. My eyes scanned his beard. It was well kept except for the scruff on his neck.

He noticed my scrutiny and lifted a brow. "What?"

"Nothing. You need a shave."

"I have a beard."

"Yes, but you need to clean up the growth on your neck."

He rubbed a hand over his throat. "I don't have time."

"I can do it for you."

"What?"

I rolled my eyes. "I've done it a hundred times. Where's the bathroom?"

"He led me down the hall to his ensuite bath. He didn't have any shaving soap, but he came up with a razor.

"Stand still," I ordered, and made do with his hand soap. He stood patiently while I lathered his skin, then, with a few quick strokes, cleaned him up. I could feel his eyes on me, but I refused to let them affect me, knowing if I did, my hand would shake. Finally, I was through. "There. Much better."

He turned and leaned toward the mirror, his hand stroking over the bare skin. "Not bad. Thanks."

"You're welcome."

An hour later, we walked on the plane and found our seats. Lobo grabbed my carryon and hefted it overhead into the compartment along with his own. My eyes dropped to the muscles that bulged under his suit coat. Then he took a seat next to me.

The flight was half empty, and we had no one near us. I looked over at him.

"I suppose we should get the details straight."

"Details?"

"Of how we met. That sort of thing. If I'm going to play your girlfriend, we need to know things about each other. At least the things your family would know."

He shrugged. "Okay. Where did we meet?"

I studied him. "My car broke down, and you stopped to help. I bought you lunch to pay you back. You asked for my number, and the rest is history."

"What kind of car do you drive?"

"Corvette. Used. I don't have that kind of money."

"No? I thought you were the most expensive escort on the Strip."

I glanced around. I hated when clients said those things out loud in public. "Look, there are things I don't talk about in public. I'm sure you're the same in your… line of work."

"Oh, right. Sorry."

"Don't let it happen again."

"Got it. So, what was wrong with your car?"

"Flat tire. The simpler we keep this, the better."

"Okay. Where did we have lunch?" he asked.

"Garcia's on Fourth Avenue."

"What did we order?"

"I had Pollo a Las Rajas, and you had tacos." I said the first things that came to mind.

"Right, because I'm a simple guy, huh?"

"You want to have burritos?" My voice was a little aggravated.

"No, no. Tacos are fine."

"The simpler, the better."

"Your meal isn't simple."

"No one would expect me to eat tacos, would they?"

His eyes swept over me. "Suppose not. Then why did you take me to a taco place?"

The ridiculousness of this conversation hit me. "Where would you like me to take you?"

He shrugged. "I don't know. Maybe I'm worth a steak."

"Okay. We went to Maury's Steakhouse. Feel more appreciated now?"

"I do. Thank you." He grinned, and I burst out laughing.

"You're a trip."

He cleared his throat. "So, how many dates before you gave it up?"

"Who's going to ask *that?*"

"My brother, I'm sure."

I rolled my eyes. "A gentleman doesn't tell."

"Maybe I'm not a gentleman."

"Maybe this time you will be."

He shrugged. "Guess we both know the real answer."

I lifted my chin and stared straight ahead.

"Hey."

I met his eyes.

"It was glorious, darlin'." He winked.

It had been. I'd said as much in my note. Did he remember? Is that why he used those exact words? I had a feeling this was going to be an interesting weekend.

CHAPTER THREE

Hope—

After changing planes in Dallas and a flight delay, we arrived in New Orleans late in the evening. By the time the Uber pulled up at our destination, it was almost midnight.

The Christmas decorations in this neighborhood were lovely, and the homes appeared to be nineteenth century mansions. I frowned. "Where are we?"

Our driver had been schooling me on how the locals say New Orleans.

"N'Wah-lins," he repeated for me.

I chuckled at his big smile in the rearview. "No, silly. What neighborhood?"

"Dis be da Garden District, darlin'."

I stared out the window at the gorgeous Grecian style home with its grand pillars and second story verandas. A fountain sparkled in front, twin red and green lights shone on it. Little white lights lit the trunks of the oak trees and holly garland draped the wrought-iron fence.

On the black gate that enclosed the walk leading up to the house was the monogramed letter B emblazoned in gold gilt.

Lobo climbed from the backseat and extended his hand. I stepped out while the driver got our bags from the trunk. Lobo pulled a money clip from his slacks and peeled off the fare and a tip.

The driver nodded. "Thank you, sir. Would you like me to carry your bags to the door?"

"That won't be necessary. Thank you."

He touched his cap. "Have a merry Christmas."

I stared at the house with my mouth open. "Wow. It's gorgeous. This is where your family lives?"

"My grandmother owns the place, but come Christmas, everyone descends."

"So, your family has money?"

"They do. I don't."

"I see. What does the B represent?"

"Broussard.

"So, you're a Broussard."

"I am."

"What's your first name? I'm sure it can't be Lobo."

"It's Laurent."

"Laurent Broussard," I repeated, more to commit it to memory than to tease.

"See why I left all this behind?"

"Because you didn't like your name?" I turned to look at him, thinking that was ridiculous.

"One of the reasons. It's a pretty crappy name."

"I like it."

"You're a rotten liar, Miss Hill." He took my hand and guided me through the gate and up the walk. He rang the buzzer, and soon shadows moved behind the glass panes.

Warm light spilled out as the door swung open to a beautiful entryway with marble on the floor and a large crystal chandelier overhead. A stern looking older man with graying hair stood peering down his nose at us. He was well dressed in slacks and a red cardigan over his button-down shirt. His eyes drilled into Lobo's.

"Your mother and grandmother are already retired for the

evening, Laurent. You'll have to say your hellos tomorrow over the morning repast. You should have arrived sooner." He stepped back without a word of actual greeting, and I frowned, studying the way Lobo's jaw tightened. He gestured me in, and I stepped across the threshold.

"Hope, this is my father, Claude Broussard. Father, this is Miss Hope Hill."

He lowered his head in a nod that accompanied a slight bow. "Miss Hill. So nice to make your acquaintance, though the timing could have been better." With that, he threw his son another glare.

I was skilled at putting men at ease, so naturally I let the charm kick in. "I do apologize for our lateness, Mr. Broussard. Our flight was delayed in Dallas, and we were at the mercy of the airline. I'm sure you understand." I slipped my hand on his arm. "It's so good to meet you after our taxing journey. It was simply draining, and I'm sure I must look a sight. I do hope you forgive us."

He patted my hand. "No worries, my dear. And call me, Claude." He even managed a smile until his eyes shifted to Lobo, and it faded away. "Your mother has had the two rooms on the third floor prepared for you and Miss Hill."

"Hope, Claude. Please," I insisted.

"Hope, then," he conceded, and patted my hand again. "And what a lovely ray of sunshine you are in this dreary home."

"Dreary?" My gaze traveled over the beautiful décor and the magnificent Christmas tree behind him. "Why, from what I see, your home is exquisite."

"Thank you, my dear. Once Lobo shows you to your room, please feel free to explore. I'm sure you're famished. Help yourselves to anything you find in the kitchen. Now if you'll both excuse me, I'm retiring as well. Please lock the door, Laurent."

With that, he turned and trudged up a staircase.

Lobo bolted the door and grabbed both our bags. "You have a talent. I've never seen him warm up that quickly to anyone."

"Never?"

"Nope. Come on." He led me up to the third floor, which consisted of a small landing and three doors. It felt like we were up in the eaves of the home.

Lobo pointed to the center door. "That's the bathroom. I'll let you take your pick of rooms."

I opened the door on the right. It was a lovely feminine room decorated in hues of soft blue and pale yellow. A set of French doors led out to what I assumed must be a balcony.

I checked the other bedroom. It was lovely in silver and grays. It, too, had French doors, and I wondered if they led to the same shared balcony.

"I'll let you have this one," I said, turning to smile at Lobo. "It's more masculine."

He rolled his eyes. "Sure it is."

I chuckled. "Did you live here?"

He dropped his bag and carried mine to the blue room. "Nope. Just stayed here during the holidays."

"Which room was yours?"

"Gran put all us rowdy kids out in the carriage house."

"There's a carriage house?"

He threw open the glass doors, and I followed him out onto the balcony that did, in fact, connect with his side. He pointed to a large shadowy structure beyond a quaint stone courtyard. "There."

"How magnificent."

"It may be now. Back in the day, it was pretty rustic."

I breathed in deeply, catching the scent of citrus. "What is that?"

"Gran's Satsuma trees. See those?" He pointed to some small trees in large terra-cotta pots on either side of the carriage house.

"They're like small oranges. Delicious. They're blooming early this year. Usually they don't until late winter, but it's been mild this year."

I stared at the starry sky. "It's so beautiful here."

"You've barely seen anything yet. You hungry?"

"Starving."

He jerked his head. "Come on. Let's raid the kitchen."

We snuck down the stairs, and I followed him through the hall and into the kitchen. Huge, tall windows with heavy crown molding filled two walls, but everything else in the room was modern.

Lobo yanked open one door of the double-sided huge refrigerator. "What are you hungry for?"

I peered over his shoulder. "What do you have?"

"Hmm. Looks like I can scrounge up the ingredients for a couple of shrimp Po' Boys. Ever had one?"

"No. What's a Po' Boy?"

"Only the most delicious sandwich ever invented. Here. Take this." He handed me a bowl of fried shrimp, a jar of mayo, and a tomato. He grabbed up some other items, and we carried them to the island. Before I knew what he was about to do, he grabbed my waist and hefted me on the counter. "Take a load off, watch, and learn."

I giggled and stole a shrimp, popping it into my mouth while he found a cutting board, some French bread, and a bread knife. I chewed, moaning around the flavorful breading and watched him slice the loaf open.

Then he began assembling his creation. "Legend has it the Po' Boy was invented during a streetcar strike in 1929. With all the drivers and motormen manning the picket lines, a local restaurant vowed to serve the workers for free. They needed a hearty, inexpensive sandwich, so they came up with this. When strikers came to the backdoor to claim one, someone in the kitchen took their order by yelling, 'Here comes another poor boy!'"

I pulled my head to the side and stole another shrimp. "Is that true?"

"So the story goes." He tapped my hand. "Quit. There won't be enough for the sandwiches."

I giggled around a mouthful. "Sorry."

"The original contained mashed potatoes, gravy, and spare bits of roast beef. Nowadays we make them with different ingredients, the most popular being seafood. But the bread is the most important part. It needs to be crispy and flaky on the outside and soft on the inside."

"You take your French bread seriously."

"Damn straight, sugar." He filled the bread with heaping portions of fried shrimp. "Once you've got whatever meat or shellfish you're using, you dress it up with all the fixins." He added lettuce, tomatoes, mayo, and hot sauce. "Like pickles?"

I shook my head.

"Me, neither."

Once he assembled it, he pressed the top down and sliced it in half, putting one on each plate he retrieved from a cabinet. Then he helped me to my feet, his hands lingering for a moment before he gathered the plates. "Follow me."

We entered a formal dining room with a table long enough to seat a dozen guests. I sat to the left of the head, where Lobo set his plate.

He remained standing. "I'll rustle us up something to drink. Be right back."

A minute later, he returned with two tall glasses of lemonade.

I bit into my sandwich and moaned around the mouthful. "Mmm. This is so good."

Lobo grinned. "Glad I haven't lost my touch. Haven't made one in years."

I watched him eat. There were things I wanted to ask him, like why his father was so cold to him, but I didn't want to ruin the delightful meal we were sharing. I glanced at the slim Christmas tree in the corner, and he followed my gaze.

"You'll find one in practically every room, each with a different theme. My grandmother goes a little nuts at Christmas."

"I love that. I would totally do the same if I had a big place like this."

"Yeah, it's all magical until it's time to pack it away."

"Don't be a grump."

He sipped his drink, ignoring me.

"Do you not like Christmas?" I asked in all seriousness.

He shrugged. "It's all the expectation, I suppose. It's like setting yourself up for a let-down."

"How can you not love Christmas?"

"Maybe it's dealing with family that gets to me."

"Do you not get along with your family?"

"Not many. I mainly came home to see my grandmother."

"Tell me about her. What's she like?"

"She was the one person who believed in me—the one person I knew would always have my back with a kind word or a bit of encouragement, even when I'd gone astray. I guess that kind of thing really sticks with a person when they don't get it from their parents."

"It sounds like she's a special lady."

"She is."

"And your grandfather?"

"He passed on years ago."

"I'm sorry."

Lobo nodded and took another sip of his drink. Then looked at his glass. "You want something stronger? I know where the good stuff is kept."

"I suppose… if you're having one."

He stood and walked through an archway into the next room, and

I could see him fixing drinks. When he returned and set the glass in front of me, I looked back.

"What's that room?"

"My grandfather's old study. Gran still keeps the bar stocked in there, especially when family descends." He lifted his glass in a toast. "Here's to hoping we get through the next few days with this charade."

The reminder made me sad. I hated we were putting this over on his family, especially at Christmas, but it wasn't my business. In my line of work, I'd seen it all. I'd been hired by recently divorced men to make their exes jealous. I'd been hired by CEOs to make their competitors jealous. I'd been hired as a date for reunions to make a man look more successful and his old buddies envious. I'd been hired to attend functions with men who didn't want to show up at alone. I couldn't judge Lobo's motives. I clinked my glass to his, making my own toast. "To a wonderful holiday."

"A wonderful holiday. We'll see."

I sipped my drink, contemplating his cryptic remark, but changed the subject. "What is this?"

"Sazerac. The cocktail of New Orleans. Like it?"

"I do."

Lobo leaned on his elbows and swirled his drink, staring into his glass before lifting his eyes to me. "So, should we talk about the elephant in the room?"

I stilled, my breath slowing. I knew we'd get around to it, eventually. Best to get it over with. "I suppose."

"Why did you run out that morning?"

I wet my lips. There were a million lies on the tip of my tongue, but I supposed he deserved the truth. "I'd felt something with you I hadn't expected. I won't say it scared me, exactly. It was more that I knew if I stayed, it could go somewhere. I didn't have time in my life for a relationship. It would just get in the way." I shrugged. "So, I guess

I did the cowardly thing and ran. I'm sorry. That wasn't fair to you."

He was silent, considering my words before he drilled to the one part I wished he'd let slip. "What had you felt that you hadn't expected?"

"You were different. I felt at ease with you in a way I hadn't felt with a man before. I felt a connection with you." I busied my hands, brushing imaginary crumbs from the tablecloth. "Perhaps it was one-sided. Perhaps it was silly of me."

"Not at all." He reached out and stilled my nervous motions. "And it wasn't one-sided. Not by a long stretch. I felt it too, that connection with you."

I met his eyes and read the seriousness within them.

"Why do you feel a relationship would get in the way? Of what?"

"My goals."

"And what are those?"

I sipped my drink, trying to decide if I wanted to share.

"Tell me."

"It's not like I want to do what I do forever. It's not a girl's dream, after all. There are other things I want to do."

"Like what? Go to school?"

"It's not important."

"Of course it is."

"Okay. I'd like to start my own business. Hopefully, that will become a possibility soon."

"What kind of business?"

"Perhaps I'll tell you before we return to Vegas."

He smiled at the promise of my words. "Mysterious. That's okay, you can keep your secret. For now."

I smiled, relieved he wasn't going to pressure me into sharing things I wasn't ready to share. "Good to know."

He grasped a lock of my hair between his thumb and fingers,

rubbing it. "Soft as I remember."

The reference to our night together brought a ton of memories flooding back. He'd been gentle with me, and I'd needed that.

"You had the saddest eyes that night. I just wanted to wrap you up and protect you."

Once again, his words hit the mark, and I didn't know how to respond.

"You'd looked… vulnerable… and soft and feminine. You drew me like a moth to a flame. There was nothing fake or coy about you."

"You were direct, and that was refreshing. I hate when men play games."

"I thought of you for a long time afterward."

"Did you?" My gaze dropped to his mouth, and I remembered what a good kisser he was, and I wanted to kiss him again. He must have read the signals I was giving off, because a moment later his hand cupped my jaw, and his thumb dragged over my lower lip.

"You have the sexiest mouth, sugar." Then his lips descended onto mine, and I welcomed them.

The kiss was soft, exploratory, like two long-lost lovers reuniting. Is that what we were? Did this mean anything? Was he taking what he thought was included in my fee? I'd explained it all to the man who'd hired me, but I wasn't sure how much of that was communicated to Lobo. Was this what he expected? God, I really didn't want that to be true. The thoughts filling my head had me pulling back.

He frowned. "What's wrong, Hope?"

"Nothing. I'm tired, and—"

"Bullshit. What's wrong?"

We might as well get this cleared up now. "I don't want there to be a misunderstanding. This isn't what I do. Sex isn't included as part of the fee I charge."

His jaw hardened. "I didn't think it was."

"I... I didn't know if you were expecting—"

"I wasn't expecting anything."

"Good. Then we're clear."

"Very clear, Miss Hill."

"I've upset you."

"No, just reminded me this is a job for you." He stood and gathered our plates. "It's getting late, and you're right. We should get some sleep. I'll take care of these; you should go on up."

"Let me help."

"I've got it. Goodnight, Hope."

I watched him retreat, and my eyes slid closed. This was the part of my job that really sucked. It would never be easy to get a man to believe what I felt was real, or to trust that what he said was true.

I blew out a breath and went to bed.

CHAPTER FOUR

Lobo—

I tapped on Hope's door at 8:00 am the following morning.

"Yes?"

I leaned a shoulder against the frame. "Breakfast is served in half an hour. I wanted to give you time to get ready."

"Oh. Thank you."

I heard her scrambling around the room and grinned, imagining her hopping on one foot and trying to get ready. The door opened, and she stared at me, her hair all tussled, a short robe belted around her waist, and a travel case clutched to her chest. My eyes trailed to her long, tanned legs and bare feet. "Bathroom's all yours."

"Thanks."

"I thought we might take a ride to the Quarter and see the sights since you've never been to New Orleans. You bring any jeans?"

"Um, no. Why?"

"You got anything suitable for riding?"

She frowned. "You mean a motorcycle?"

"Yeah. I might be able to swing a loaner from the local chapter."

"Oh."

"You okay with that?" I couldn't tell from the way she bit her lower lip.

"Sure. I'll find something."

The way she said it sounded like she was trying to please a client, and that was the last way I wanted her to think of me. I should have

NICOLE JAMES

told Daytona this whole idea was insane. "I'll meet you downstairs."

"Okay. I'll try to hurry."

I turned and trotted down the three flights, hearing the shower come on. I tried to scrub the image of her naked body, all wet and soapy, from my imagination. When I entered the dining room, my father and mother were already sipping coffee at the table.

"Laurent," my mother said, rising from her chair, her face filled with happiness. She held her arms out, and I moved into them. She only came to my shoulder, and I dipped my head to kiss the crown. The scent of magnolia blossoms enveloped me and hurtled me back to my childhood. It was her signature perfume and one I would always associate with her.

"Bonjour, Maman. It's good to see you," I whispered against her head.

She gave me a squeeze in return, then pulled free to meet my eyes. "Where is this girl you've brought home?"

"She's a woman, not a girl, Maman, and she's getting dressed. She'll be down soon."

"A late sleeper, hmm? Your grand-mère won't be happy about that."

"Well, I don't see her at the table yet, either." I heard a cane tap on the floor.

"I am never late." My grandmother's voice was soft, but clear. "Qui est-ce? Can this be my favorite petit fils finally home to visit his favorite grand mère?"

I turned and smiled, taking in her frail stature. She was more stooped than the last time I'd seen her, but it had been ten years and time and age had taken its toll. I knew she was ailing, but for almost ninety, her eyes were clear, and her mind was still sharp as a tack.

I clasped her hand in mine and kissed it, then both cheeks, as was our custom. "It's good to see you, Grand-Mère. You're looking very

50

pretty this morning."

She gave me an accommodating smile. "Still the charmer, I see."

I led her to her seat at the head of the table and pulled out the chair.

"Merci, Laurent." She leaned her cane against her knee.

As if on cue, the woman who'd been her cook and servant for more than forty years entered from the kitchen with a cup and saucer.

"You're café au lait, Miss Jacqueline."

"Thank you, Estelle, dear."

I poured myself a steaming cup from a silver coffee server on the sideboard and moved to a seat. Before I could pull out the chair, my grandmother patted the lace tablecloth to her right. "Sit here, Laurent."

My father's eyes followed me from the opposite end of the table. His lips were pursed as he took a sip from his own bone china cup. It rattled when he set it in the matching saucer.

"Claude! Be careful. This set has been in the family for generations."

"Then may I suggest you reserve it for special occasions?"

"I will do with it as I see fit, with no advice from you. Est-ce que tu comprends?"

Oh, my father understood all too well. His mother had been correcting him as far back as I could remember. I hid my smile behind my cup, but it was too late. He'd seen it, and that only frustrated him more. He snapped his copy of the Times-Picayune closed and stood.

"If you'll excuse me, I have work to do." He headed down the hall.

"Work?" My grand-mère cocked a brow. "You left the firm when you turned sixty."

"Maman, please. Don't start. It's the holidays, and Laurent is home."

"He knows how I feel about his papa, don't you?" The old girl actually smiled and winked.

I couldn't hold back the chuckle. Movement in the doorway caught my eye, and I looked up to see Hope standing there. My gaze swept over her. She was dressed in black leggings and an off the shoulder sweater and black ankle boots.

"Good morning." She smiled, taking in the people gathered.

I rose to my feet. "Grand-Mère, Maman, may I present Miss Hope Hill. Hope, this is my grand-mère, Jacqueline, and my mother, Cecile."

Hope moved around me to extend her hand to my grandmother. "I'm so pleased to meet you, Mrs. Broussard. Laurent speaks fondly of you so often. I feel like I already know you."

My grandmother's eyes shifted to me. "Has he?"

"Most definitely. Thank you for welcoming me to your lovely home. It was very gracious of you to extend the invitation to share the holiday with you. And may I say how stunningly beautiful I find all your Christmas décor."

"Merci. That is very kind." My grandmother's gaze shifted to me with a new light in her eyes, and I knew she was pleased with the woman I'd brought home.

Hope moved to my mother's chair and clasped her hand. "It's lovely to meet you, Mrs. Broussard."

"Call me Cecile." She nodded to a chair. "Please, sit. Did you sleep well?"

"Yes, the bed was quite comfortable. I slept like a baby." She took the seat I held out.

Her manners were impeccable, and I couldn't help wondering if this was all part of the service that made her so successful.

Estelle came in carrying a platter of ham and another of cream cheese crepes with strawberry compote.

"Strawberries! My favorite." Hope exclaimed with a big smile.

My grandmother's face lit. "Really? Then I'm sure you'll enjoy this dish. It's one of my favorite breakfast entrees. Estelle fixes it for me often, don't you, dear?"

"Yes, ma'am. Even if I do have to use frozen strawberries this time of year." Estelle dipped her head to Hope. "It's from the Broussard family recipe book."

Jacqueline nodded to the dish. "Please, try some. Laurent, serve your guest."

I picked up the platter and did so, then held it for my grandmother to serve herself.

Hope moaned around her first forkful of the flavorful entrée. "Oh, my." She covered her mouth. "Oh, that's delicious."

Grandmother nodded, studying the two of us. "Then you shall have the recipe so that you may make it for my Laurent when you are married."

My hand tightened around my fork, but I tried to show no emotion.

Hope, though, covered for us both gracefully, playing her part like a pro.

"I would love to have it. It would be an honor to learn one of your favorite family recipes." Her smile shifted from my mother and grandmother to me. "I'm sure Laurent would love that."

She hadn't lied, but she hadn't corrected them, either. It was something I felt the need to do. I knew it was the height of irony to be picking bones about something like that when our entire relationship was a phony. Still, it didn't sit well to have them think there was a wedding on the horizon.

"Grand-Mère, don't get ahead of yourself. You'll be the first to know if I have any plans to celebrate."

She, of course, did not find that amusing. "I thought you were engaged."

"I said I was bringing someone home to meet you."

That seemed to satisfy her. "Oh, I see. Get my approval, is that it?"

I was about to protest when Hope's hand covered mine. "Well, he thinks so highly of you. Of course, he would want your approval for anything so serious."

Across the table, my mother's eyes dropped to Hope's bare ring finger, then flicked to mine.

I couldn't help but put her at ease. "You'll be the first to know, Maman."

My grandmother cleared her throat, and my eyes shifted to hers. "You both will, okay?"

"Where's your father?" Hope asked, changing the subject. Thank God.

"He had some business to attend," I replied.

My grandmother harrumphed.

We ate the rest of the meal in silence.

I laid my linen napkin down and stood. "If you'll excuse us, Grand-Mère, Maman, I planned to show Hope the Quarter today."

"Of course. You're excused. Be sure to show her the cathedral."

I nodded and led Hope out of the room.

"You ready?" I asked in the foyer, grabbing up a black backpack I'd carried down.

"My purse is upstairs."

After she ran up to get it, my brother and his wife walked in with my five-year-old niece.

His eyes widened when he saw me. "Laurent. I thought they were kidding when they said you were coming home."

"Julien." We gave each other a back-slapping hug. My eyes dropped to the little girl I'd never met. I squatted down. "And this must be Suzette.

She did a little curtsy, holding her dress out, and I glanced up at her mother. "Teaching her young, huh?"

"Of course." Her mother's face lit with pride.

I stood and embraced her. "Olivia."

She squeezed me tight. "It's good to have you home, Laurent."

Hope skipped down the stairs and came to a halt. I stepped back and presented her. "Hope, this is my brother, Julien, his wife, Olivia, and my niece, Suzette."

"How lovely to meet you all." She put her hands on her knees and leaned down, smiling at Suzette. "Why, that's the prettiest dress I've ever seen. Yes, ma'am, it is."

Suzette gave her a shy smile and twisted from side to side, her skirt flaring. Then she looked up. "You're under the mistletoe. That means you have to kiss."

I glanced at my brother's grinning face. "It's the rule."

Hope gave my hand a tug, and I turned and dipped my head, giving her a peck.

My brother huffed out a laugh. "Don't act like kissing your gorgeous girl is a hardship, brother. Are you leaving?"

"We were just headed out to catch the streetcar. Thought I'd show Hope the Quarter."

"Ah, the Quarter. Well, don't let us keep you."

"We'll see you tomorrow for the cookie contest?" Olivia asked.

I rolled my eyes. "Are they still doing that?"

"It's the best part," Suzette informed me.

I couldn't help but smile and tap her nose. "Then we wouldn't miss it for the world."

She giggled.

"Julien, is that you?" my grandmother beckoned from the dining room, and it was my brother's turn to roll his eyes.

"Duty calls."

I slapped his shoulder. "But the crepes are good."

He chuckled and led his family into the dining room.

I held the door and followed Hope outside to the gate. We walked a block to the nearest streetcar stop and waited with two other people.

"What's in the backpack?" Hope asked, lifting her chin to it.

"My cut and helmet." When she frowned, I knew I had to elaborate. "My leather club vest."

"Why did you bring that?"

"I never ride without it on. Club rules."

"Are there a lot of rules to follow?"

"About a dozen."

She eyed me, cocking her head. "Somehow, I wouldn't have pegged you for a man who followed the rules."

"I'm not, but some things are worth it."

"I see." Her eyes drifted to the street sign with two sets of beads wrapped haphazardly around the top, then shifted to the trees to find more. "What's with all the beads?"

"Mardi Gras. People toss them. They get hung up on a lot of things down here."

"And no one takes them down?"

"The city's more worried about the ones that land on the ground than what gets caught in the trees. Those are the ones that end up in the storm drains, clogging up the sewers. Nowadays, at every parade, there are strategically placed recycle bins for revelers to dispose of their unwanted beads after the celebrations. It's made a world of difference."

"How do you know so much about it? I thought you hadn't been home in years."

"I haven't. Doesn't mean I don't keep up with the news."

She cocked her head. "Do you miss it?"

"Home?" I shrugged. "Parts of it. I miss the city, the culture." I waggled my brows. "The food."

She laughed. "I can certainly understand that."

"Where's home for you?"

"Oklahoma."

"No shit."

"Thackerville on the very southern edge. Population about four-hundred people, but we had three casinos, and I once heard if you divided up all the slots and gaming machines to the population, there'd be twenty for every person."

"Wow. That's crazy."

"We used to drive the eighty miles to Dallas every chance we got when I was a teenager. Of course, my mother never knew that."

"I see you escaped the small-town life."

"Started working at one of the casinos when I was old enough. My looks helped me get the job. Of course, it also invited unwanted attention from all the pit bosses. Once I had learned enough skills—"

"You moved to Vegas," I finished the sentence for her.

"Exactly."

The streetcar rolled down the tracks toward us, its bell clanging. The front was decorated with green garland and red velvet bows. We boarded and scooted onto one of the wooden seats.

"This is so cool." Hope smiled.

I studied the happiness on her face, and felt joy at showing her a town she'd never been to before. I only hoped she'd be as cool when I introduced her to some of my New Orleans chapter brothers.

CHAPTER FIVE

Hope—

We crossed Canal Street and strolled down Bourbon, passing restaurants, bars, a few X-rated clubs, and souvenir shops. I paused in front of one shop, taking everything in.

"You want a souvenir?"

I eyed the multitude of things for sale. Mardi Gras masks in green, gold, and purple, creole cookbooks, chicory coffee, pralines, hot sauces, a million items with either fleur-de-lis or alligators emblazoned on them, from t-shirts to keychains. A display of feather boas that took up the entire left wall caught my eye.

Lobo noticed my interest. "You should get one."

I moved closer. It would be a fun souvenir. "Which color?"

"Whatever you like."

In the end, I chose a red one and brought it to the counter to pay. Lobo pulled it from my hand and laid it on the counter, then tossed two wrapped pralines on top.

"My treat."

"Thank you."

When we exited, he unwrapped one of the pralines and passed me the other. "Ever had one?"

"No."

"They're my favorite."

We walked a couple more blocks, and Lobo steered me through a courtyard entrance.

"You have to have a Hurricane in Pat O'Brien's courtyard."

A waitress seated us at a black wrought-iron table. Lobo waved off the menu. "Two Hurricanes."

"Of course." She smiled and left.

I glanced at the nearby fountain surrounded by ferns. "That's so pretty."

"You should see it at night. It's lit up with colored spotlights, and the urn in the middle burns with a tall flame like an Olympic torch."

"Wow. That would be something to see."

Birds chirped in the small trees around the perimeter. One pecked at the stone tiles. The sound of the fountain carried to me.

"It's so peaceful here. It's like the outside commotion on Bourbon Street doesn't even exist in this hidden gem."

"It's a popular spot for that exact reason." He pulled out his phone and tapped a text. "I'm hoping someone in the club can loan us a bike."

He set his phone aside when the waitress brought our tall, iconic glasses. I sipped from my straw.

"Yummy."

Lobo smiled. "Glad you like it. So, what did you think of my grandmother?"

"I liked her. But what's the deal with your father?"

Lobo folded his arms and rested his elbows on the table. "My ol' man is a piece of work. It's stuff that goes back to when I was growing up. Fathers expect a lot out of their sons. I never lived up to expectations. I got over it."

His phone rang, and he picked it up off the table, glancing at the screen. "Excuse me, while I take this."

"Of course."

He stood and moved through the brick archway onto the side street.

While he was gone, my phone dinged. I replied to my text, then slipped my small planner out of my purse and made a notation.

I sipped on my drink and stared at the job I'd just confirmed. Once I would have been pleased to have this appointment, now there was almost dread.

I felt a presence at my back and looked up.

Lobo leaned over my shoulder, peering at what I'd written.

"Who's Mr. Black?"

"What?" I closed my planner and shoved it back into my purse.

"New Year's Eve 7:00 pm. Mr. Black."

"A client," I answered. I could tell he didn't like that, and from the look in his eyes. I wasn't going to apologize for it. He knew what I was when he hired me.

A thunderous roar sounded, and I recognized it as motorcycles. The rumble of their pipes echoed off the walls of the tightly packed eighteenth-century buildings of the Quarter.

Lobo downed the rest of his drink, still standing, then met my eyes. "The boys are here. Drink up."

"I'll never finish this."

He motioned our waitress over. "Can we get a *go cup*, doll?"

"A go cup?" I frowned.

"So you can take your drink out," Lobo explained. "That's what we call 'em down here."

"Sure thing." The waitress walked to the bar area and returned with a plastic cup, transferring my drink to it. "Here you are. Enjoy."

"Thank you."

Lobo led me out the side street entrance. A line of bikes four car lengths long took up the space from us to the corner of Bourbon, their rear tires backed to the curb.

"Wow."

Leather-clad men stood on the walk, stretching and lighting up cigarettes. Lobo grabbed my hand, and we walked toward them.

He greeted an older man with dark hair graying at the temples. "Undertaker, how are you?"

The man turned. "Lobo. Good to see you, brother."

They clasped hands like arm wrestlers and backslapped each other.

Lobo stepped away to introduce me. "Undertaker, this is Hope Hill, a friend of mine. Hope, this is Undertaker, president of the local chapter."

I extended my hand. "Nice to meet you."

His hand swallowed mine. "Welcome to New Orleans, darlin'. I hear it's your first trip."

"It is."

"How do you like our fine city so far?"

"I love it. It's beautiful."

He chuckled, glancing at my go cup. "I see you're already up on one of the traditions. Go cups. They should be allowed everywhere. Am I right?"

"I won't argue with that. It is nice to take it with me." I sipped on the aqua straw.

Undertaker was introduced to several men, then we all moved inside the bar. It was almost like a shotgun style house, long and narrow. Tall French doors opened onto the street, with white hurricane shutters propped wide. A long ornate bar dominated the left wall and tables and chairs took up the right, with a narrow aisle in between. We sat on stools at the bar.

I stuck with my Hurricane, but Undertaker bought Lobo a drink. "So, home for Christmas, huh?"

"Yep. First time in ten years," Lobo replied.

"Place hasn't changed much, has it?"

"No, sir."

They talked about motorcycles and other things, and I drifted to the door to watch the passing crowd. A younger club member came to lean on the door frame next to me. "How're you doin', darlin'?"

"Just fine. Thanks. I think I've fallen in love with this town." I watched the tourist moving past. "I'm Hope, by the way."

He held out his hand. "They call me So Cal."

I shook it and arched a brow. "For Southern California?"

"Bingo. That's where I'm originally from. But I've been here for a long time. How about you?"

"Oklahoma."

He arched a brow. "Seriously?"

"I know, right?"

He chuckled. "You know, every time I hear the name of that state, I think of that line by Louis Gossett Jr in An Officer and a Gentleman. *Only two things come out of Oklahoma, boy*—"

"Oh, yes. I remember." I stopped him before he finished the infamous line.

He laughed. "You raise steers out in Oklahoma, Hope?"

"Not me. I was a townie. Except it was a one-stop-light town, so I got out of there as fast as I could."

"Don't blame you there. You comin' out to the party with us later?" he asked.

I frowned. "What party?"

"My brother, Joker's place. He's havin' a little Christmas party. We're doin' a secret Santa." He leaned closer. "I got Undertaker's name. I got him a box of Viagra."

I giggled. "Oh, really?"

"Yeah. Don't tell anybody."

I made an X on my chest. "Cross my heart." Then I pretended to lock my lips and throw away the key.

He chuckled and pointed his finger. "I knew I liked you. A

woman who can keep a good secret."

"Oh, I'm definitely one of those."

He drained his beer. "You want one?"

"No thanks. I'm still working on my *first ever* Hurricane."

"First ever?" He waggled his brows. "Gotta love a virgin."

Then he winked and strolled to the bar.

A few minutes later, I felt a presence at my shoulder and turned, smiling, expecting it to be either So Cal again or Lobo. It was neither. I didn't know this man. He wasn't part of the club. He was maybe mid-twenties and looked like he may have been drunk.

"Hey, pretty lady." The beer in his cup sloshed over, and I stepped back. He put a hand on the door frame behind my shoulder. "You just get to town?"

He smelled like booze and made a grab for my arm, but I yanked it free. Suddenly So Cal was back, shoving the man aside.

"Beat it, punk."

A bar stool crashed to the floor, and I jerked my head around in time to catch Lobo bolting toward us. The next thing I knew, he had the kid by the throat and shoved him against the door frame. "You don't mess with this lady. You don't talk to her, and you sure as fuck don't touch her. Understand?"

The guy was so drunk he laughed and waved his hand, muttering, "Okay, okay. I was just being friendly."

"No one here wants to be your friend. Look around, dumbass. What do you see?"

His watery eyes moved over Lobo's shoulder. "Bikers."

"That's right. Now get the fuck out. Go home and sober up. Only warning you're gonna get. I see your face in here again, they'll be bringing an ambulance for what's left of you. Got it?" Lobo shoved him out onto the sidewalk.

The man stumbled but caught himself before he went over the

curb.

"Good thing you didn't fall on my bike, dumbass," So Cal called after him. "I wouldn't have been as polite as my brother here."

The man stumbled down the street, totally oblivious to his surroundings. I'd been hit on before by drunks, by frat boys, by conventioneers, by lonely divorced men… It was never pretty. They always seemed quite pathetic, but whatever drove them to the bottle, I couldn't fix for them.

Lobo stepped closer. "You okay?"

"Yes, of course. That really wasn't necessary. He was harmless."

"Never underestimate any man. They all have the potential to be trouble. And you're wrong. That was absolutely necessary. Bottom line, no man harasses you or puts their hands on you without your permission. Not while I'm around."

"Thank you."

"You're welcome. Come and sit at the bar with me."

"Sure."

I finished my Hurricane, and Undertaker bought me another rum drink. "Best to stay with one liquor, darlin'," he'd warned.

So Cal sat on my other side. "Sorry about that. I shouldn't have abandoned you."

"You didn't abandon me."

"I saw the guy at that table over there. He'd been watching you. I shouldn't have walked away. Or I at least should have warned your ol' man."

"My ol' man?"

"Isn't Lobo your ol' man?"

I didn't even know what that meant. I thought I did, but I didn't want to get it wrong, so I made a vague response. After all, I was in town to play the part of his girlfriend.

"He brought me home to meet his family."

"That sounds like *Serious Town* to me."

I laughed. "You're a hoot."

"You got a sister looks like you, Hope?"

"Sorry. No."

"Damn. Just my luck."

I heard Undertaker speaking to Lobo on my other side.

"We're headed to Joker's. He's got a sweet setup on the water. Converted a barge into a house. You got time, you should come with us."

"Where is it?" Lobo asked.

"Not far. Irish Bayou. We take I-10 almost to the Twin Span bridge and hang a right just before we cross the Ponchartrain. It's a mile or two down on the left. It's a nice ride and a pretty day for it."

"Sounds great." Lobo glanced at me. "You up for it?"

"Sure."

"Good." Undertaker tossed back his drink and stood. "Let's roll, boys!"

Up and down the bar, stools scraped across the worn wooden floor as men drained their glasses, and everyone headed outside.

Undertaker pulled a key from his hip pocket and handed it to Lobo, then pointed to a bike. "The Road Glide at the end is yours to use."

"Great. Thanks."

We moved to it, and Lobo passed me the helmet dangling off the handlebar. Then he pulled his own helmet out of his backpack and shoved the pack in one of the hard-side saddlebags.

Once our helmets were strapped on, he threw a leg over the big bike and lifted it off its kickstand, firing it up. He patted the seat behind him. "Climb on, babe."

I scooted on, my black stiletto ankle boots finding the pegs.

He slid on shades and passed me a spare set. "Hang on,

sweetheart."

I put my hands on his waist.

He patted my thigh, twisting to look at me. "You ready?"

I gave him a big grin, excitement swirling through me. "So ready."

He chuckled, then waited until the others were all mounted and fired up. They pulled out in pairs, and we fell in at the end. It wasn't easy maneuvering in the tight streets of the Quarter, but these men made it seem so. Their riding skills—Lobo's included—were next level.

We roared up an entrance ramp onto the expressway, and the bike surged forward as Lobo hit the throttle. Soon the pack of bikes were zooming northeast on I-10 headed toward Slidell.

CHAPTER SIX

Hope—

Twenty minutes later, the line of bikes slowed and turned into a small gravel lot.

Lobo parked next to the others, and I scrambled off the back and looked around. I spotted some houses up on stilts across the street. The smell of the musky swamp water of the bayou hit my nose.

There was indeed a houseboat built on a barge moored, what looked like permanently. A gangplank led up aboard the barge.

We followed the others up the planking and onboard.

A large deck was nicely decorated with lovely patio furniture. There was a nice seating area with a pretty rug and in another area, a large patio table under a covered pergola. Ferns grew in pots.

"Wow." I took it all in.

"Nice, huh?" Lobo said at my shoulder, his hand claiming my elbow. "Come on."

We followed the others inside. A stunning mural dominated one wall. There was an open floor plan living room, dining room, and modern kitchen with a big island.

"I love this place!" I squeaked.

Undertaker introduced us around. "Joker, this is Lobo from the Nevada chapter and his lady, Hope."

He shook hands with Lobo and nodded to me. "Welcome. Grab yourself a beer or a drink. The bar's over there. We also have coolers set up outside. We're grilling some food soon." He looked to me. "The girls have a daiquiri bar set up in the kitchen if you're up for one."

"Sounds great."

Joker emitted a sharp whistle. "Holly, come meet our guests."

"You've got a beautiful place here, man. Undertaker told us you built this all yourself." Lobo glanced around.

"It turned out well. Now I'm in business doing conversions like this for clients."

"That's fantastic."

A pretty blonde approached me. "Hi, I'm Holly. Joker's ol' lady."

"I'm Hope, Lobo's girl."

"Nice to meet you, Hope. Come with me, and I'll introduce you to the girls."

I followed her to the kitchen area and met several of the women. I tried to keep their names and faces straight. Cat was Blood's ol' lady. Paige belonged to Wicked, AJ was Undertaker's ol' lady, and Skylar was Undertaker's daughter and Shade's ol' lady. Jessie was with Ghost, and Tink was with Hammer. They'd come down from the Alabama chapter. Then there was Mama Ray, the unofficial mom of the club.

Holly pulled me to the side and told me her ol' man had been killed years ago, and now she took care of "her boys" as she called them.

The ladies had two blenders going.

"What'll you have, Hope? We've got the classic lime and also strawberry."

"Strawberry, please."

She smiled. "That's my favorite, too."

I soon had a frozen drink in my hand, complete with fresh strawberries on a skewer, and was chit chatting with the girls. I was fascinated by them. They all seemed like strong, independent women, but yet they loved their men and were devoted to them and this club.

"Love the man, love the club," Cat said. "They're a package deal with this bunch."

"I see that," I murmured, looking through the sliders out to the deck where the men had naturally migrated near the grill.

"How long have you been with Lobo?" AJ asked.

"Not long. Is it obvious?"

She smiled. "Kind of."

"Do you like riding?" Holly asked

"This is the first time I've ridden. Out here today."

"Wow, you really are a newbie to all this," Jessie said.

Skylar grabbed the pitcher of strawberry daiquiris. "Know what that means, ladies?"

Tink hooked my arm. "Time to fill her in."

"Let's move to the back deck where we can have some privacy from the men." Holly nodded for us to follow.

Paige winked. "Good idea. Don't want them to hear everything we're going to tell you."

***

Lobo—

Blood, Shades, and Ghost gathered around me, interested to hear about the Nevada chapter.

"How are things going? Had any more problems with the Death Heads?" Shades asked.

"We've taken care of that for the time being, but with that bunch it's like playing Whac-A-Mole, you know? We think we're done with them, and they pop back up again."

"Ain't that the truth? We've had our own dealings with them. Haven't we, Blood?" Ghost lifted a chin to the man and met my eyes. "They took him captive years back. Held him for days, shot through the side and burnin' up with fever."

"Yep." Blood nodded and stared at his longneck. "If it wasn't for Cat, I wouldn't have lasted another day."

"What happened?" I asked.

"They decided they didn't want me dying just yet, so they kidnapped her from the hospital parking garage, where she worked as a nurse. She was terrified when they thrust her into the room with me and locked the door. She saved my life, though, and we escaped. Now she's my ol' lady."

"Man, that's wild. What a story to tell your kids, huh?" I met his eyes.

The corner of his mouth pulled up. "My daughter thinks it's goddamn romantic. I blame her mother for that. My son thinks I should never have let them get the drop on me. Teenagers. Go figure."

"So, you've got two kids, huh?" I asked.

Ghost chuckled. "Hell, we've all got kids. Pesky teenagers, and my boy's the worst. The next generation is fixin' to take over. Kick all us old-timers out," he joked.

"Who you callin' an old timer, asshole?" Blood smirked.

Ghost slapped his chest. "You, old man."

Shades dipped his head to light a cigarette, then studied me through the trailing smoke. "You got kids?"

"Not yet. Want some, though."

"Think twice about that, bro. My daughter, Rebel, keeps me up at night worryin' about all the shit that could happen to her."

"Lock her in a room," Ghost suggested.

"That ain't always the answer. Just 'cause it worked for you with Jessie," Shades replied.

Blood chuckled. "Damn. I remember that like it was yesterday. I let her loose and brought her to the gun range, remember?" He studied the tip of his cigarette. "Taught her to shoot. She was a damn fast learner, too."

"Yeah," Ghost said, his voice dripping with sarcasm. "Thanks for that."

Blood chuckled. "Figured she's shoot you, and I'd steal her away."

"You had no shot with her," Ghost insisted.

"Guess we'll never know. I'm happy as a clam with what I got now, so water under the bridge."

Ghost lifted a brow to me. "You believe this guy?"

I grinned.

The others began talking about replacing the timing belt on somebody named Sandman's bike later, and I tuned it out.

Ghost jerked his head, and I followed him to the cooler. He reached in and grabbed our refills, then leaned against the railing. "So, this chick your ol' lady?"

"Hope? No."

"Why not? She's stunning, brother."

"The truth would shock the hell out of you."

"Well, hell, let's hear it."

"I met her a while ago. Just a one-night-stand. She was sitting at this high-class bar in one of the hotels on the Strip."

"Frequent those often, do ya?"

"What I was doing there is a long story. Anyway, I spot her, looking gorgeous in this sexy little black dress. Some old dude started pawing her, so I walked over and ran his ass off. One thing led to another, and she leads me up to this gorgeous penthouse suite. Right away, I'm thinking either this chick is loaded or there's a man in the picture somewhere."

"Which was it?"

"I'm getting to that. So we spend one phenomenal night together. Next morning, I wake up and she's gone. Fast forward to about a week ago. My president finds this invitation on my counter to a Christmas ball back home in New Orleans. Wants to know if I'm goin'. I tell him I don't want to show up without a woman. See, I promised my grandmother next time I came to town I'd be in a relationship. She's wanted me married with kids for years now."

"Grandmothers are like that. They lay the guilt on you."

"Daytona gets the wild idea he's going to hire someone to be my fake girlfriend. I bring her home. Gran dies a happy woman. Everybody's happy."

"And?"

"The paid escort who shows up on my doorstep turns out to be Hope."

His brows lift. "No shit?"

"I kid you not."

"And how's that been workin' out?"

I shake my head. "The temptation is gonna kill me."

"Wait. Back the train up. She doesn't put out?"

"Not that kind of escort. Which, hey, I'm glad. I like this girl, and our chemistry was off the charts. Now I'm stuck *pretending* it's real."

"When, in fact, what you're feelin' is real?"

"Bingo. I'm fucked."

"Is she interested?"

"That's just it, see? She's so damn good at what she does; I don't know if it's all for show or just an act."

"Yeah, that's a tough spot you're in." Ghost turned and leaned his elbows on the rail, looking at the setting sun. "Want to know what I think?"

I paused with the longneck halfway to my mouth. "Do I?"

"Just make a play for her. You'll find out real quick if she's for real."

"I don't want to fuck up this weekend. It's only Wednesday. We don't fly out of here until next Tuesday, the day after Christmas."

"I see your point." He slapped my shoulder. "I still think it's worth a shot. But I guess only you know if she's worth that risk."

CHAPTER SEVEN

Hope—

It was getting late, and above us was a sky full of stars. I sat curled up in the corner of the pit group with a toasty blanket wrapped around me, staring at the small fire Joker had built. Most of the group had left, except for the Alabama group. I heard they were staying at Undertaker's place.

The girls were in the kitchen, and Lobo was talking with some of the men over by the table.

Ghost wandered over with a beer and a Santa hat on his head. "Mind if I join you?"

"Not at all."

He sat about two feet away and put his boots up on the glass coffee table, then stared at the fire.

"Is it safe to have a fire on a boat?" I asked.

"The barge is made of iron and steel, so I'm guessing we're safe. It flares up and sets that windsock on fire, run for the gangplank."

I giggled and stared at the hat. "Cute."

"Climb on my lap, little girl, and tell me what you want for Christmas." He waggled his brows, then pulled the cap off. "I'm joking with you, doll. Hope you know that. Right?"

"Yeah, I get that."

"Good. Because I'm a happily married man. Love my ol' lady to pieces. And she'd cut me in pieces if I ever hit on another woman."

I nodded. "Now that I've met Jessie, I believe that may be true."

He chuckled. "So what do you think of this bunch of rabble? We're not so bad, huh?"

"You're all good people. I've been having a great time."

"Glad to hear it. You know, you ever get serious about that guy"—he tipped his beer toward Lobo—"you'd probably should know some stuff."

"Like what?"

He twisted toward me, adjusting his head on the backrest to stare at me. "So, you are interested."

I sucked my lips into my mouth, afraid I'd spilled the beans.

"Don't deny it. I see it."

"And if I was?"

"First thing, don't be afraid. This is a family, and we take care of our own. Not gonna lie and say shit doesn't hit the fan sometimes, because it does, and when it does, you gotta be strong. But the good times far outweigh the bad. Wouldn't be a member in this MC if they didn't."

I stared at Lobo.

"He treat you right?" Ghost asked in a low voice.

"Yes. I mean, we… um, haven't known each other that long."

"You sticking around long enough to figure that out?"

"I don't know. It may not be up to me."

"It's up to you. That boy over there"—he pointed to Lobo again—"he wants a shot. A real shot. Maybe you feel the same, you two should make the most of the time you got. See where it goes. What have you got to lose?" With that, he stood. "Merry Christmas, darlin."

I sat and thought about his advice. I was afraid I had a lot to lose. My heart, for one.

The party wound down and soon we were the last ones.

"Why don't you two stay in our guest room?" Holly offered. "It's a long way to the Garden District, and you've been drinking. Besides, the temperature's dropping, and Hope doesn't have any leathers."

Lobo looked over at me.

"Um, well, if you're sure it's no imposition?"

Joker yawned and threw an arm around his wife. "None at all, sweetheart. It's down the hall past the fridge. Night."

They disappeared inside, and Lobo tugged my hand, turning me to him. "You sure? We can head back if you want. Hell, I can always call an Uber. Might take them a while, though."

"I'm fine." I dropped his hand and cupped his face. His expression gave away his surprise and perhaps a bit of confusion. "Do you remember what I said that first night while we were eating?"

"About this not being part of the deal?"

I nodded. "Can we forget about the arrangement? Can we pretend it's like the first night we met?"

"What are you saying?"

"Can we give this a real chance?"

He searched my eyes. "Are you sure? Because I'd really like that."

I smiled. "Then kiss me like you mean it."

He caught my mouth, reminding me all over again just what a good kisser he was. Then he took my hand and led me to the guest bedroom. It was small, but the bed was a queen, tucked against the wall with wooden bookshelves all around and a mirror behind the headboard. A door to the side led into an ensuite bathroom, but what caught my eye were the sliding doors that led out to a side balcony overlooking the water.

"It's beautiful. I can see the moon." Its shimmer lit a path across the water.

Lobo stepped behind me and pushed my hair out of the way, giving his mouth access to my neck. He trailed soft kisses along the curve.

"I've wanted to do that all night."

Sighing, I leaned against his chest.

"I've thought about you a million times since that night in Vegas," he whispered.

"I have, too."

"Cussed you out a million times, too, for not leaving a name or number. I wanted to see you so badly."

"I'm sorry, but I'm here now." He turned me around and cupped my face.

"This isn't fake anymore. It never has been for me, Hope. Even that night, everything I felt was real." Then he brought my mouth to his, and his tongue swept inside. He groaned in the back of his throat, and I felt the vibration in my mouth. I stepped closer, pressing my body against his, needing to feel every inch of space between us gone.

We'd been apart for so long, seemingly lost to one another, yet in a way it was like no time had passed.

His hands clutched my ass and gathered me even tighter against him until I felt the proof of his desire between us. Then his fingers trailed up my sides, gathering the hem of my top with them and sweeping my sweater over my head with a whoosh.

His eyes dropped to my gold lace bra that matched the color of the sweater. He dragged a knuckle over one cup, brushing over my already hard and aching nipple. I reached behind me and unhooked it, dropping it to the floor and giving him access to my bare breasts.

"I used to lie awake at night and ache for your touch, trying to remember every moment of our time together."

"I did, too, baby. For the longest time I was pissed I hadn't gotten a shot of you naked and wet in that bathtub. I swear I would have jacked off to it every night."

He dropped to his knees, bringing his head level with my breasts, and took one nipple into his mouth.

I threaded my fingers into his hair, holding him there and loving

80

every sensation. A thrill of desire and need shot from my nipple to my womb, and I moaned, my head falling back.

His mouth moved to the other nipple, giving it the same attention. Then he got to work yanking the zippers on my ankle boots.

"I love these boots. They're hot as hell on you."

"Thanks." I clung to his shoulders for balance. When he was done, he hooked his thumbs in the fabric at my waist and stripped me of both my leggings and panties all in one motion.

When I was naked, he stood, grabbed my waist, and tossed me on the bed. I bounced and grinned, coming up on my elbows. "Undress for me, handsome."

He shrugged out of his cut and lay it across the dresser, then peeled his thermal shirt over his head, revealing that gorgeous chest.

Next came the belt buckle. There was something about watching this man unbuckle his belt that got me wet every time. I licked my lips. His eyes dropped to my mouth while he unzipped and pulled out his erection. It was long and thick and hard. Just like I remembered.

It didn't take him long to kick his boots off and finish stripping. The man was on a mission. Soon he put a knee in the bed and climbed his way up my body. When his weight came down on me, and his hot skin pressed to mine, I sighed and wrapped my arms around him.

We were finally together again.

I knew without a doubt I never wanted to let him go.

His mouth captured mine in a long kiss. He chased my tongue. He alternated between soft and wild. He came back again and again, changing positions of his head, licking my lips, then diving in for another taste.

One rough palm glided over my hips and stomach, and two fingers dipped between my legs, finding me wet. God, yes, I was wet for this man. Wet and ready for him. But as hot as we were for each other, somehow I knew he wasn't going to rush this. He was going to draw out every moment. What we had was too good to rush, too good to be over quickly.

I was so needy for him, but I got on the same page, letting him set the pace and taking what he gave.

His fingers toyed and his thumb coaxed my clit out from hiding. It was eager for him, too.

Lobo stared into my eyes while he took his time playing with me. "You like that, baby?"

"Yes," I breathed, running my hands over his muscled arms and back. I couldn't stop touching him. I wanted to familiarize myself with every inch. I followed the lines of a particularly colorful tattoo.

He held my eyes still. "You pick a spot, I'll put your name there. Hope. Your name has a lot of meaning. You've given me hope for the future, something I didn't have a few days ago."

He went motionless. "Is that your real name?"

"Hope is. Hill is not. My real name is Hope Kowalski."

"Good. So, Hope still works for that tattoo. Anyplace you want, babe."

"I'll take you up on that." I pulled him down and kissed him. I liked everything he was saying—loved it, in fact, but I needed to come. I'd longed for this, for him. When I tore my mouth from his, I urged him on. "Take me, Lobo. Make me yours. Please."

His eyes gleamed in the moonlight coming in through the sliders. He reached to the floor and pulled a condom out of his pocket and rolled it on. Then he moved over me, spreading my legs with his knees. "Wrap around me, babe."

I was eager and did so immediately. He circled my wet pussy once, twice, then plunged inside, groaning as he did so.

"Fuck, I missed you." He pressed his forehead to mine and began moving, slowly at first, letting me adjust to the fullness of his thick cock inside me. Then building speed, until his body curled over mine, muscles tensing, rocking forward with each thrust in and out. His chest glistened with sweat, and his lungs bellowed in and out.

He reached a hand between us and stroked me until I was bucking against it, needing it. I climbed rapidly toward orgasm. "I'm almost there."

"Hurry, baby." He dipped his head and sucked hard on one nipple. That zing sent me rocketing over the edge with a stuttered breath and a long moan.

He pumped a few more times through my orgasm, then followed me over the edge into ecstasy, growling in my ear.

"Fuck, yes, baby."

A moment later, he collapsed, and I welcomed his weight. I clutched him to me, trailing my hands across his slick skin, up and down his spine, then threading my fingers into his hair.

He lifted and kissed me, then bumped his nose to mine and his eyes crinkled with his smile. "The girl's still got it."

"The boy's got it, too."

He chuckled and rolled to his back, dragging me against his side and stroking a big palm down the curves of my waist and hips. He smacked my ass. "Best lay ever."

I giggled and burrowed close, loving the feeling of lying with him. It didn't last long. He pulled his arm out from under me and went to deal with the condom.

The bed felt empty without him. I realized I didn't want to be apart from him, even for a moment. How crazy was that? I was like a teenager in the throes of her first love. Was that what this was? Did I love this man? I wasn't ready to go that far just yet. But I was happier than I could ever remember being. If that wasn't love, what was it? This was more than lust. I knew that to the bottom of my soul.

He returned and cuddled me close again, turning to face me. He held me this way for a long time, then tapped my hip.

"Roll over."

I did as he asked, smiling to myself. He liked to spoon. He fit his body around me and wrapped his forearm across my waist. His hand played with my boob, and he trailed kisses from behind my ear and down my neck. Eventually, his hand strayed to between my thighs, and he gave me another orgasm before telling me to sleep.

It didn't take long for me to drift into contented slumber.

CHAPTER EIGHT

Hope—

The car pulled away as we pushed through the entryway into the foyer.

"Come join me for breakfast." Lobo's grandmother called from the dining room.

Lobo looked at me apologetically, but I waved him off. He grabbed my hand, his warm, rough fingers wrapping around mine, and led me into the room.

"Good morning, Grand-Mère." Lobo leaned over and kissed her head.

"Yes." She eyed us with a knowing smile. "Seems it was a good morning, or should I rather say a good night?"

"Grand mére," Lobo called out, seemingly appalled his grandmother was hinting at us sleeping together.

"So, where were you two last night?"

"Lobo took me to meet some of his friends. They had a party on a barge. It ran kind of late." I smiled sheepishly.

"Well, eat some breakfast and then go clean up. Everyone should arrive in the next couple of hours."

"Everyone?" Lobo questioned.

"Yes, today is lunch here and then the Broussard Family Cookie Decorating Competition."

"Uh, that's right." Lobo rolled his eyes.

"Oh, you hush." She swatted at his hand. "Everybody else enjoys it, and you know I love playing the role of judge."

"Fine. I'll be good, but I'm not decorating cookies."

"I know, I know. Even Eve could never get you to participate."

Lobo's jaw clenched at the mention of this name, but I didn't ask and his grandmother didn't seem to notice his change in demeanor.

"All the grandchildren and their families will be here for lunch, except Delphin. He's getting in a little later. Your parents went into town to do some last-minute shopping, but they should be back by then."

Lobo nodded but seemed no longer interested in the conversation.

We quickly ate and hurried off to get showered.

***

The rest of the family started trickling in about an hour later. The first to arrive was Lobo's brother, Julien, his wife Olivia, and daughter Suzette. I was thankful because we'd already met them on our way out the door yesterday, so it relieved some of the pressure.

Julien and Lobo seemed to have a good brotherly bond. Olivia was quiet, more observant, but kind.

"You ready to meet the whole family?" she asked in a soft voice.

"I think so."

"Just remember, Grand-Mère is really the only one who matters, and she seems to like you, so keep your chin up."

The words were meant to ease my nerves, but they seemed to be a warning that some of the family would give me a hard time.

The doorbell rang again, and this time a beautiful blonde woman, round with child, came through. She looked like a goddess; pregnancy glow definitely suited her. When her eyes connected with Lobo, her face lit up, and she ran into his arms. A pang of jealousy surged through me until they separated, and Lobo called, "Hope, I want you to meet my little sister, Rosalie."

My cheeks blushed slightly. "Hello, nice to meet you."

"Nice to meet you too, Hope." She waved away my hand and pulled me in for a hug. "You're the first girl my brother has brought home in years, so I think we should skip straight to hugs."

I returned her smile, but guilt washed over me at the ruse. They thought me someone important, but I didn't even know exactly what I was to Lobo.

Rosalie turned and gestured to a man who walked in behind her, carrying a young girl. "This is my husband Beau and our daughter Marie Claire."

"Nice to meet you." I smiled at the blonde curly-haired girl clinging to her father's neck.

"She's a shy one." Rosalie rubbed her hand down her daughter's back.

"That's okay. I was a shy one, too." I winked at her and earned a tiny smile in return.

The last to arrive was a tall woman with dirty blonde hair perfectly styled in long loose waves and a tall blonde man who looked like a walking Ken Doll. As a matter of fact, they both looked like they belonged in a department store catalog.

"How are you doing?" I heard Lobo's whispered breath in my ear.

I leaned into him. "I'm good."

Out of the corner of my eye, I saw the gorgeous woman approach us, her husband trailing behind.

"Hello, Laurent." Her voice purred like a lover.

I studied them both. I could tell something from the past hung between them.

"Eve." Lobo returned the greeting, but his voice seemed cold. "This is Hope."

Eve's head turned to me as if noticing me for the first time. Her gaze dropped to where Lobo had entwined his fingers with mine. "Nice to meet you."

She seemed anything but pleased to meet me, but Lobo squeezed my hand, and that was all I needed.

"No, no, the pleasure is all mine." I plastered on a serene smile.

"Well, I'm Marcel, since no one's going to introduce me. Eve's husband and Laurent's cousin." He held out his hand.

"I'm Hope."

He released my hand and turned his attention to Lobo. "Laurent, been a long time."

The words seemed like the sort of thing you'd say to a friend you missed, but they came out more like a statement of fact than anything conveying feelings felt.

"It has."

"Lunch is served," Estelle announced to the bustling room.

The long dining table had been set like a five-star restaurant, and the aromas had my mouth watering.

"Estelle, what is that delicious smell?" I asked as I entered.

She smiled proudly. "That's bacon-wrapped shrimp and grits you're smelling. But there's also a spinach and strawberry salad, and I got some bread pudding cooking in the oven."

"Well, it smells divine."

She bowed her head, still smiling as I claimed my seat.

Rosalie sat across from me. "So, tell me how you two met."

Lobo glanced my way for a brief second before telling the story we had prepared.

She continued to ask questions about us that made me uneasy. Typically, it wouldn't bother me at all, but I noticed how Eve hung on every word. It felt almost like she was looking for cracks.

As lunch disappeared from our plates, the conversation turned to the competition, and I was thankful.

"We need another for the last team. Laurent, you in?" Rosalie asked.

Lobo looked appalled. "Absolutely not. Never participated before and don't plan to start now."

Rosalie's shoulders slumped. "Well, someone has to compete alone, then."

"Nonsense, I'm sure Hope can do it. Right? You're not afraid of a little competition." Eve smirked.

"I don't think—" Lobo started to decline for me, but I tapped him on his chest.

"No, no babe. I can compete." My eyes bore into Eve.

"Great!" Rosalie squealed, oblivious to the tension building. "I'll text Delphin and let him know."

"Delphin?" Lobo gave Eve a look that said I know what you're up to.

"What? We already decided. I'm sure they'll do fine."

I looked to Lobo, trying to understand why being partnered with someone named Delphin was going to be a problem.

***

A couple hours later, I was dressed in a frilly apron that looked to be more for aesthetics than practicality. The mysterious Delphin arrived. I examined him closely as he entered the foyer. His hair was immaculate and his outfit impeccable. He bantered back and forth with his brother Marcel. But when he greeted his brother's wife, Eve, he was standoffish and made me feel like our distaste for her was a commonality.

It wasn't long before he made his way over to me.

"So, you're the unlucky one who got stuck with me? Delphin."

He held his hand out.

"Hope," I replied, taking his in a gentle shake.

He leaned close and flashed a set of perfectly whitened teeth. "You must have pissed off somebody to get stuck with me."

"I believe that would be Eve," I whispered back.

He lowered his voice to match mine. "Then I've found my new favorite person. How'd you end up on her bad list?"

"I'm not sure. Lobo—" I paused when I spotted the look of confusion on Delphin's face and corrected myself. "I mean, Laurent introduced us, and she's been an ice queen ever since."

"Laurent?" He chuckled. "You came with Laurent?"

I nodded, wondering what he found funny.

"Say no more. That's why she hates you."

"Why?"

His eyes sparkled at the realization that he'd get to spill the gossip. "Well, she's his ex-fiancée. He's the one that got away. That, and any chance at getting Grand-Mère's heirloom necklace. Laurent's always been her favorite, so whoever marries him will inherit the thing. Even Rosalie knows she'll never get it." Seeing the worried look on my face, he waved it off. "Don't worry, Rosalie doesn't care one bit. Neither does Olivia."

"Well, that's a relief." I glanced to where Rosalie stood talking to Lobo, wondering why he didn't mention Eve was his ex. "Maybe we'll just have to show Eve up."

He deflated at the suggestion. "Unfortunately for you, we have our work cut out for us."

I chuckled. "Are you telling me you're not a cookie decorating champion?"

"Far from it. I may look fab in an apron, but that's as far as my decorating skills go. I usually get put with one of the kids, but even they've learned they don't want Uncle Delphie on their team."

"Oh, you can't be that bad." I swatted playfully at his arm.

"Last year we decorated Christmas sweater cookies and mine ended up looking like I massacred a family. We had to hide them from the kids."

I burst out laughing, earning glares from Eve.

"Well, I have a feeling we're going to do just fine this year." I patted his arm reassuringly. "I may have a talent for this kind of thing."

A flare of hope shone in his eyes. "You mean to tell me I might actually win that godforsaken gingerbread man trophy?"

"Let's just say we have a chance."

"I'll take it." He hooked his arm in mine and led me toward the large kitchen. As we passed Lobo, Delphin called out, "I think you may have a gem here!"

Lobo nodded in agreement as we brushed by. "Good luck."

The kitchen was massive. A large island stretched across the middle, the length of an oversized dining table. Three of the walls were lined with granite counters, making it look like it belonged in a restaurant, not someone's home.

There were five stations spread throughout the room. Each had their own set of supplies-mixing bowls, frosting, icing, sprinkles in every shape and color, spatulas, icing bags, and tips. They clearly took this competition seriously.

The teams each claimed a station: Eve and Marcel, Rosalie and Marie Claire, Olivia and Suzette, Beau and Julian, Delphin and me.

Grand-Mère entered, carrying a gold-colored cup with a gingerbread emblem emblazoned on it.

"The competition rules are as follows. You can work with any of the materials provided. You each get one tray of twenty-four cookies to decorate. The team with the best decorated cookies after two hours wins. I, of course, am the judge and have final say on whose cookies look the best. The winners' cookies will be served at the annual

Christmas ball and take home the Gingerbread man trophy. Any questions?"

Everyone remained silent.

"Then you may begin."

The kitchen immediately came alive as the teams created their plans.

"Seems unfair that the other teams are family members who could have been planning designs for weeks," I grumbled.

"Yes, well… They don't expect us to win anyway, and the cookie shape is always a last-minute surprise. So, what's our plan?"

I tapped my chin, mentally inventorying our supplies. The tray of cookies was a combination of trees, snowflakes, and snowmen.

"Okay, I'm thinking we make these trees look like real pine trees with fluffs of snow on their branches, complete with a cardinal sitting on a single branch. The snowflakes will be all white with ornate piping, giving them the illusion of actual crystallized snowflakes, and the snowmen will be traditional black top hats with red scarves and a dusting of pink on their cheeks."

Delphin opened his mouth and shook his head. "I did tell you I massacred sweaters last year, right? How do you expect me to do whatever it is you just said?"

I smiled at him sweetly. "I don't. I'll do all the piping. I need you to mix colors."

"Okay." He nodded, as if convincing himself he could do this. "Okay."

One hour into our time, we had white iced all the cookies for a base layer, and I had already piped the snowflakes, adding three pearl shaped sprinkles into the center of each one.

Delphin had already mixed a bowl of brown and evergreen colored icing. He was now working on a vibrant red.

I slowly piped the brown trunk up and down the tree cookie and three branches sticking out on either side. I was grabbing the green to cover the branches in pine needles when Delphin huffed.

"Look at her over there, taunting me with that smirk."

I glanced at Eve. "Well, then she can choke on one of our cookies."

"Girl, you're bad." He pointed the spatula at me, flicking his wrist. "And I like it."

My laugh tinkled out, and I glanced behind me again to see her eyes narrowed. She probably thought we were laughing at her, and I guess we kind of were.

"What happened anyway?" I asked. "Why'd they break up?"

Delphin shifted and seemed uncomfortable, which was a contradiction to how he responded to spilling gossip earlier.

"Look, I like Laurent," he said as he dished the red into a piping bag the way I had shown him. "He's always been really good to me, and I like you, too, but I don't think I can share his secrets. He'll have to be the one who does that."

I nodded, not liking that answer but respecting it.

He brought the red over and set it next to me. "Girl, those look like legit pine trees."

I grabbed the white piping to add the fallen snow to the branches. "Can you grab the sugar? I want to add it to the snow, so it looks like it sparkles."

"Sure thing." He moved off to grab some.

Right before I started piping, my chair was bumped, and I quickly pulled up to avoid squeezing a dollop of white onto the tree. I glanced over my shoulder, expecting to see Delphin apologizing, but instead saw Eve.

"Oh, I'm so sorry. Did I do that?" She sneered.

"Don't worry, you didn't do anything. Shouldn't you be at your own table?" I questioned rather loudly, causing the nearby teams to glance our way. She blushed under the scrutiny of the watching eyes and mumbled something about their sprinkles rolling across the floor.

"Back to work then, don't you think?"

She turned on her heels and marched across the room. I turned to my cookies, but not before seeing Olivia sneak me a thumbs up.

Someone called a fifteen-minute warning, and I added the final touches to each cookie. Delphin even brushed gold powder onto the Christmas tree star toppers.

"Time's up," Grand-Mère called from the doorway. We all backed away from our cookies and studied our competition.

The guys' cookies weren't bad, but definitely looked homemade. Olivia and Suzette went with blues and golds. Rosalie and Marie Claire had made pink snow ladies, pink trees filled with glittering sprinkles, and even pink snowflakes. It made me smile; pretty sure Marie Claire's favorite color must be pink. Eve and Marcel seemed to be our biggest competition. Her trees were snow covered as well and even had a cardinal.

"Wonder where she got that idea," Delphin whispered angrily in my ear. "You should call her out."

"Hey, she's your sister-in-law," I whispered back.

"Don't remind me."

Grand-Mère moved through the room quietly with an unreadable expression. Lobo and his parents slid into the room to watch the awarding of the winners. When she finished, she picked up the trophy and, with a twinkle in her eye, announced, "Everyone did a wonderful job, but one team stood out above the rest. I'm sure all would agree Delphin and Hope are our winners."

Delphin pumped his fist into the air and cheered. Laughter broke out around the room, as well as congratulations.

Confusion filled Lobo's face, and he moved closer to look at our tray. His confusion turned to an impressed look. "Well, aren't you full of surprises? These look amazing."

"Did you doubt me?" I laughed.

"Never." He leaned forward and wiped some frosting from my cheek and then put his finger into his mouth, licking it off. "Delicious."

"Is it?" I watched his mouth.

"You tell me." He leaned down, placing a warm kiss on my lips.

"Delicious." I beamed back.

Over his shoulder, I saw Eve huff and exit the room.

Lobo seemed to be over her, but I didn't think she felt the same.

***

Lobo—

I was so proud of Hope. She really was making an effort to fit in, and I knew it wasn't easy with this bunch. I brought her hand to my mouth and kissed it.

"Come, everyone. Dessert and coffee are served in the dining room," Estelle announced. I helped Hope out of her apron and waited while she washed her hands, then led her into the dining room.

Hope breathed in the aroma of what was being served today. Two large platters sat on the sideboard, with dessert plates and silver spoons set out for us to help ourselves. We got in line with the others.

"Mmm. It smells amazing." She leaned toward Rosalie.

My sister spoke low over her shoulder. "It's Creole Bread Pudding with Bourbon Sauce. Another of the Broussard family recipes. The other is Doberge Cake. Estelle always makes it for me. She knows it's my favorite." Rosalie patted her rounded stomach. "Plus, I can't have the bourbon sauce."

I dipped my head and added, "But you get to eat for two, so win-win."

Eve came out of the kitchen and took her place at the end of the line, picking up a plate and spoon. I turned to Hope and gave her a kiss on the temple.

"What was that for?" she asked.

"Just because."

A loud shriek from the kitchen drew all our attention. "Oh, no!"

Estelle came rushing out. "I'm so sorry, Mrs. Broussard. I went to the pantry to get the packaging to wrap up the cookies, and when I came back in the kitchen, the tray was on the floor. I swear it was on the counter. I have no idea how this happened."

Grand-Mère walked to the kitchen, the family behind her. When we pushed through the doors, the beautiful cookies Delphin and Hope had made were in crumbles all over the tile.

Hope stared at the floor and pain flashed across her face, but she quickly masked it.

I glanced behind me at the rest of the family. Eve stood at the back, a smug look on her face.

"It's okay. I can make another batch," Hope suggested.

My grand-mère took her hand and patted it. "You are an angel, dear."

Eve's expression turned to stone.

CHAPTER NINE

Lobo—

After the contest, I sat with a cup of coffee at the dining room table, talking with my sister's husband, Beau, and my brother, Julien.

Eve and Marcel had left immediately after dessert. She was nothing if not the world's biggest sore loser.

Hope and Delphin were decorating another batch of cookies, and everyone else was cleaning up.

The topic had turned to Saints football, like it usually did when the three of us got together.

"There are so many layers to the Saints' current situation." Julien leaned on his elbows.

Beau lifted a brow. "True. But, at some point, reality has to set in, and they're just not a good football team this year."

"That's obvious," I agreed, sipping my coffee.

"That's the cold, hard truth." Julien nodded, his head dropping to stare at the tablecloth.

"Why do you think that is?" I asked.

Beau threw his hands in the air, as if it were plain as day. "They're undisciplined. They lack energy. They're wildly inconsistent in their execution. The list goes on."

"Yep," Julien agreed. "It all adds up to a 3-7 team that, frankly, deserves to be right where they are."

Rosalie came through the swinging door from the kitchen. Her eyes hit her husband, and they seemed to exchange some silent communication.

He stood. "Hey, Julien. Can you give me a hand with something?"

"Sure." My brother downed his coffee and followed him out of the room.

Rosalie approached me. I knew my sister like the back of my hand, and I didn't like the look on her face. Something was going on with her. I just wasn't sure what it was. It was almost Christmas. She had a career she loved, a husband I knew she was crazy about, and a beautiful child. What could be bothering her?

She slipped into the chair next to me.

I frowned. "What's wrong?"

"Can we talk in Grampa's study? I don't want the family walking in on us."

"Sure." I scooted my chair back and followed her, stopping in the center of the room, and turning to see her pulling the old pocket doors closed. She looked shy and nervous as she approached, her fingers lacing. "Rosalie, what is it? Are you okay?"

"I'm fine." Then she pivoted and paced away. "That's not true. I'm not fine. This thing's been eating me up inside. I've wanted to talk to you about it for the longest time, and now you're here, and I've got to say it."

"For God's sake, what's the matter?"

"I never should have let you take the fall for me all those years ago."

I dragged a hand through my hair and spun. "Not this again. I did what I needed to do. End of story. Rehashing everything does nobody any good."

"I'm so sorry, Laurent. I'm so sorry." She broke into a sob, and I caught her to my chest, dipping my mouth to her hair.

"Shh. It's done. It's over. We all got past it. It worked out for the best."

Her head lifted, her eyes pooling with tears that spilled over and ran down her cheek. "You went to prison. It ruined your life. How can you say it all worked out for the best?"

"You think I could have stood by and watched your whole life go down the toilet for one mistake? You had your whole life ahead of you. You had big plans. You were going to law school in the fall. Tulane, like Dad. It was all set. You were going to be the attorney dad always wanted me to be. They were all so proud of you. And look at you now. Married with a beautiful little girl, and a baby on the way. I'm glad I made that decision, and I'd do it again in a heartbeat."

"But what about you? It ruined your life, Laurent." She slapped her chest. "How do you expect me to live with that? It should have been me taking the punishment. Not you. Never you."

"I was your big brother. It's what big brothers do. They look out for their little sisters. I had to protect you."

"It was wrong, and I can't live with the guilt any longer."

That had me freezing solid. "What do you mean?" When she didn't answer, I grabbed her upper arms and shook her. "What do you mean, Rosalie? Don't you dare do anything stupid."

She pushed out of my arms, her face a mask of no emotion, and that sent a chill down my spine.

"You have a husband who adores you, a beautiful child, and another on the way. Don't you dare do anything to throw that all away. Don't you dare."

"Laurent, this has all been so unfair to you."

"I did the time. It's over. It's done. Let it go."

"I can't. Don't you see?"

"What are you thinking of doing?" I was afraid of her answer, but I had to know.

The wind rustled in the trees outside, and branches banged against the window. I felt the cold breeze right through the old glass panes. It matched the cold pit in my stomach. I dragged a hand through my hair and moved behind her. She stood at the front of our grandfather's desk, fiddling with a letter opener. I snatched it from her hand and tossed it down, then spun her around and tilted her face up to mine.

"Look at me, Rosalie." Finally, her eyes lifted. "There is nothing to be gained, do you understand? I have a life in Nevada now. I've gotten beyond it. Everything's good. Everything's fine."

She tried to shake her head, but my palms held her cheeks. "Everything is not fine. You just pretend it is. I see the way father talks to you. How he cuts down everything about you. I can't stand it, Laurent. It's not fair."

I gave her a tender smile. "Since when is life fair? You have a happy life and a good husband. He doesn't need to find out any of this."

"He already knows."

The smile slid off my face. "What?"

"I told him. Years ago. He knows how this eats at me. The guilt—"

"So, he knew you planned to talk to me about this today?"

"Yes."

"Who else knows the truth?"

"No one. I swear. But they should. They all need to know the real story."

"They don't. Just leave it, Rosalie. Please? For me?"

The doors slid open, and our father stood there. I wasn't sure if he'd overheard.

"Oh? I didn't know anyone was in here." His gaze moved between us, and I knew he thought it odd to find us here, so I made up a story. Seems I was good at that.

"Rosalie was just telling me about Marie Claire's ballet recital.

Nutcracker. I'm sorry I missed it." I moved past him. "I really should go find Hope. Excuse me."

Stalking toward the kitchen, I paused to take a deep breath and calm myself before pushing through the swinging door. I didn't need anyone asking what was wrong.

With a pasted on bright smile, I pushed into the room.

They were just finishing drying up the last of the baking pans. Hope's bright smile greeted me.

"How's the world's greatest cookie makers?"

Hope threw a dish towel at me. "Don't tease."

"I'm not teasing. That's what the trophy says, right?" I picked it up and read it. "Yep. Says right here."

"We're wonderful," Delphin replied as he put the last of the utensils away and turned. "I, for one, will cherish this day for the rest of my life, and I plan to make sure Eve never lives down her crushing loss."

Hope and I chuckled.

"Please do. She needed a good put down." My gaze connected with Hope. "Thanks for that."

"Hey, I'm here to help."

Delphin pulled his apron off. "Well, I've got to run, ladies." He pointedly included me in that grouping with a lift of his brow. Then he reached for the trophy. "I'll just be taking this with me. It's going over my mantle. I may not bring it back next year."

"You have to! It's the only one we've got," Cecile insisted.

"Try prying it from my cold, dead fingers, Auntie." With that, he gave a *toodle-oo* with his fingers and sashayed out the swinging doors. A moment later he returned and grabbed one of the tins of the replacement cookies they'd made. "These are mine, too."

Hope laughed and called after him. "They're the best."

I looped an arm around her neck and pressed a kiss to her

forehead. "You did me proud, babe."

She leaned into me, cuddling against my chest, and I saw the look of happiness and approval on Gran's face.

CHAPTER TEN

Lobo—

That night, I knocked on Hope's door just after everyone downstairs had gone to bed. When she pulled it open, she was dressed in a loose t-shirt, no bra, and her legs were bare. I put my finger to my lips.

"Shh. Come with me?"

She peeked out into the hall and into the darkness beyond me. "What is it?"

"It's a surprise."

We tiptoed down the stairs, then I led her through the hall and out the back door. When her bare feet hit the stone courtyard, she danced.

"It's freezing. I don't have shoes."

I bent and presented my back. "Hop on."

She did, and I carried her to the carriage house, shoving the door open with my shoulder. I set her on her feet and led her upstairs. Her mouth dropped open when she saw my handy work. I'd been up here for about a half an hour, setting everything up.

Candles were lit all around the room, and a small fire burned in the wood stove. It filled the room with warmth. Above us were open rafters, and I'd draped them in little white Christmas lights, which gave the place a fairytale quality.

There was a queen poster bed draped in netting and made up with bright white sheets and a down comforter. That and a pair of nightstands were the only furniture in the room.

"You did all this for me?"

"Like it?"

"It's beautiful."

"My shot at being romantic."

She moved against me and cupped my face, then she went up on her toes and brought her mouth to mine. My hands landed on her waist and traveled up and down her sides, slipping under the loose shirt. Her skin was warm and soft. I stopped on her ribcage, and my thumbs stroked along the underside of her breasts.

When we broke the kiss, I stared into her eyes and gathered the hem of her shirt in my hands, then dragged it up her body and over her head.

Her skin appeared golden in the candlelight.

"Perfection," I whispered.

She stood there, unmoving, letting me look my fill. I lifted a hand and brushed the back of my finger over her nipple. They both stood at attention, like she was begging for them to be touched, to be sucked.

I cupped both breasts in my hands, lifting and squeezing them, watching her reactions flicker in her eyes. Her lids dropped to half-mast, and she sucked her lower lip between her teeth.

"So pretty. Prettiest tits I've ever seen. Absolutely gorgeous." I kissed her, then bent and lifted her up. Her legs went around my waist and those pretty nipples were at mouth level. I couldn't resist taking one into my mouth while I carried her to the bed.

Her head dropped, and she pulled me closer, hanging onto my neck.

I took her to her back on the white coverlet. Her hair spread around her, and she looked sexy as hell.

I stroked one palm down her leg from hip to knee and back again. Before I could strip her of her sexy panties, she rolled us until she was straddling me.

I stroked her thighs and gazed at those pretty breasts. I reached for them, but she batted my hands and shook her finger. "Not yet. You're overdressed."

I lay and let her work the buttons on my shirt. She stroked her hands over my chest. "Sooo pretty," she teased.

My body shook with laughter, and that made her breasts jiggle some more.

I shrugged out of my shirt, and she scooted down my body to undo my belt. My dick was hard, and it got even harder watching her work my buckle free.

I stacked my hands behind my head and let her run the show.

She scooted back and pulled my pants and boxer briefs off, kissing her way across my abs.

When I was naked, she trailed kisses up my thighs, skating around my hard cock standing at attention and begging for her mouth. She made it to my navel, where my tattoos started, and her eyes locked with mine. That pretty pink tongue of hers appeared, the tip tracing the lines of my ink.

I brought one hand down and laced my fingers through her silky hair, guiding her where I wanted her. "Suck me, baby. Wrap those pretty lips around my hard cock."

She did, giving the head a few good laves with her tongue before taking it in her fist and guiding the head to her lips.

I sucked in a breath as she went down on me. My eyes slid closed, and I enjoyed every sensation. My hips lifted, and I began to slowly fuck her mouth.

When the pace picked up, I brought the other hand around and gathered her hair so I could watch my wet dick slide in and out of her lips.

I felt my orgasm building, and I knew I wasn't going to last long. I grabbed her arm and spun her, positioning her legs on either side of my head, then I jerked her panties to the side and sucked on her clit.

She bucked, but I held her tight and stroked it with my tongue. I tunneled two fingers into her pussy and found that spot that drove her wild.

It distracted her, and she pulled off my dick.

"Suck me off, baby. Don't stop."

She went back to what she was doing, and so did I. I kept at her until she was moaning around my dick and my fingers were coated with wave after wave. Still, I didn't let up.

When she was so close, she couldn't take anymore, I flipped her to her back and finished her off. Then I spun and dragged her mouth to my dick. When I was almost there, I pulled out and came all over her glorious tits.

We both collapsed on the bed.

"That was so good," she whispered, rolling her head to mine, her breathing heavy.

I smiled. "Glad you enjoyed it."

"You're still going to fuck me, right?"

I broke out in laughter. "Yeah, babe. I'm still gonna fuck you."

When I'd sufficiently recovered, I dragged her to her hands and knees, rolled on a condom, and grabbed her hips in my hands. Then I spread her legs with my knees and took her from behind.

I stroked my palm down her spine and back up and over her sexy ass. "My baby's greedy, isn't she?"

"So greedy. You gonna give me that big dick of yours?"

I grinned. "You know I am, beautiful." But first, I was going to ramp up her anticipation, so I kept stroking her skin, making her wait until the first barely there touch of my fingertips made her jump.

"Please."

"Please, what?"

"Please, give it to me."

"Give you what, doll?"

"I need you. I need you inside me."

Before she finished the sentence, I slipped two fingers inside that dripping wet pussy. I pumped in and out. "This what you want?"

She dropped her head and moaned when I found that spot again. I worked her clit with my fingertips until her entire body trembled.

"Oh, God."

"Come for me, baby."

My hand was working in a frenzy now, and she emitted a keening moan, and she coated my hands with her orgasm. She collapsed to her shoulders, her breathing heavy.

I withdrew my fingers and carried them to my mouth, licking them clean.

"I'm not through with you yet, doll." I leaned over her, one hand next to her head, and thrust my hard dick inside her drenched pussy. It fluttered around me and clenched tight.

I moaned. "Yeah, pretty girl. You want my cock, don't you?"

I slid in and out until I was slamming against her. I held her hips tight to keep her in place. A sheen of sweat covered my chest and arms. My eyes locked on her pussy, taking my cock so good. In and out. In and out. I was fascinated and couldn't drag my gaze from it.

She moaned, and her walls tightened around me.

"Fuck yes. Do that again."

She did.

I tried to hold off, but soon it became impossible. I was about to explode. I grimaced, my jaw tight. I slapped her ass, and she clamped down on me again. That was all it took, and I rocketed into oblivion, ecstasy washing over me like the finest drug surging through my veins.

My eyes slid closed, and my mouth parted as that nirvana took over. I stayed on my knees as long as I could until my drained body was out of even that much energy.

I fell to the bed next to Hope. My chest heaved. I lay there for a minute, then walked to the bathroom and delt with the condom.

When I returned, Hope scooted into my arms, and I laid my cheek on her head. "I'm exhausted."

"Me too, but in *such* a good way." I felt her smile against me, and I kissed her hair. She turned to catch my eyes. "Thank you for doing all this."

"My pleasure."

She laid her head on my chest, and I stroked her back, staring at the ceiling and thinking about what Rosalie had said to me earlier. I was afraid she was going to do something, but I didn't know what. With that in mind, I knew I didn't want Hope to be blindsided by any of it.

"Got something I want to tell you. Something that happened a long time ago. I just want you to know, in case someone says something about it."

She wrapped an arm around my waist and squeezed. "Okay."

"It happened when Rosalie had just graduated high school. I was still at home then. She'd been out with my father's car, and I was sitting outside sneaking a cigarette. Rosalie comes flying up the street and turns in the entrance by the courtyard. I stand and take in the car. It's immediately evident she's been in some kind of wreck because the car is all smashed in on the side.

"She stumbles out, and it's obvious she's been drinking. I can hear sirens in the distance and know they've got to be headed toward us. I asked her what happened.

"She told me she turned in front of a car, and it hit her. By then the sirens are coming closer, so I take the keys from her and tell her to get inside. I tell her if anybody asks, she was home all night, that I had the car out. She nodded and ran inside."

Hope squeezed my waist again, like she knew what was coming. "You took the blame?"

"She's my kid sister. She'd been accepted at Tulane. She had plans to go on to law school. Her life was all set. I couldn't let her throw it away because of one stupid night. So, when the cops pulled in, I said I'd been the one driving. They arrested me for hit and run. It was only after I got to the station, I found out the driver of the other car was dead. Next thing I know, I'm being charged with manslaughter."

I stroked my fingers along Hope's arm absently, dreading telling her the next part. "My grandfather was alive at that time. He got me the best lawyer he could, but I still did a year in prison."

"Oh my God."

"I wouldn't have done a damn thing differently, so don't feel sorry for me. I did what big brothers are supposed to do: protect their little sisters. I'm glad I did what I did."

"So, does your family know?"

"Well, evidently Rosalie told her husband at some point. I'm guessing he's known for years." I shrugged. "At the time, only Rosalie and I knew the truth. My grandfather went to his grave thinking the worst of me. Suddenly, I was a convicted felon and the black sheep of the family. Things between me and my father have been rocky ever since."

"I'm so sorry, honey."

"Like I said, wouldn't change it. Just wanted you to know."

"For what it's worth, it doesn't make me think less of you. The opposite, in fact. You did the selfless thing and sacrificed your future for someone you love. That's honorable. That's noble. I'm only sorry it destroyed your relationships."

I kissed her head. "Get some sleep. Gran's got a busy day planned for tomorrow."

She snuggled against me and settled down. Soon her breathing changed, and I knew she'd drifted off. I stared at the ceiling, worrying about things I had no control over.

CHAPTER ELEVEN

Hope—

On Friday, we arrived early for twelve o'clock mass at St. Louis Cathedral. Lobo had taken a tongue lashing for not showing it to me when he'd brought me to the Quarter, but somehow, we'd never made it this far.

I stood in front of it with his grandmother on my right. I think she was secretly pleased she got to see my reaction as I stared up in awe.

She gripped my arm, and at first I thought it was in excitement, then I glanced at her face and she swayed against me. I grabbed her elbow.

"Are you okay, Jacqueline?"

She sucked in a breath and steadied herself. "I'm fine. Just got a little dizzy."

"Maybe we should go home?" I whispered.

"Nonsense. I'll be fine."

"You're sure?"

She patted my arm, then tapped her cane. "Come. If you think the outside is something, wait until you see the inside. Laurent, escort us inside."

"Yes, ma'am." He extended his arm to us both and we followed his father and mother through the entrance. Inside the vestibule, his grandmother nodded to the rack of votive candles burning.

"Is there anyone you'd like to light a vigil candle for, dear?"

I looked over. "There is, actually."

She had Lobo obtained one for me, and I used one of the long taper sticks to light it. I closed my eyes and said a prayer. Lobo lit one as well.

"Who was that for?" I whispered as we entered the cathedral.

"My grandfather."

There was no more time to talk as we walked in. The first thing that struck me was how bright it was on the inside. I'd expected it to be very dim, like most cathedrals. While the ground level was full of ten stained glass windows, light poured in from above. "It's so bright."

Lobo's grandmother pointed toward the ceiling. "The upper portion is full of big windows letting in lots of light, dear."

I couldn't help noticing the unique checkerboard floor leading between the pews to the front of the cathedral. The black and white marble was striking.

We moved toward one of the very front pews and took our seats.

I leaned to Lobo's grandmother. "It's beautiful. Really. Truly impressive."

She patted my knee. "I hoped to see Laurent married here. I had big plans. It would have been the wedding of the decade. But when everything happened with the accident, his fiancée, as you young people say, dumped him." She stared at me a moment, then waved her hand. "Eve wasn't alone long. She threw him over for his cousin, Marcel."

I shook my head. "What kind of a woman does that?"

"I know. Very tawdry. She wasn't right for Laurent from the start. I should have run her off. Saved us all the trouble."

Mass began, and she straightened in her seat. We were unable to talk again.

My gaze traveled around the cathedral, taking in all the striking ornamentation. It really was quite breathtaking. I couldn't help but imagine walking down the long aisle myself, and Lobo standing at the alter in a gorgeous tux waiting for me, his eyes filled with love. It was a beautiful dream; I just wasn't sure it could ever become a reality.

After mass, we headed over to a nearby restaurant where Jacqueline had reserved a private room for the family to have Réveillon dinner.

"What exactly is Réveillon?" I asked her.

Jacqueline hooked my arm as we walked along.

"Réveillon means *awakening* in French. It's a Creole tradition that dates back to the 1800s. It was originally a big meal eaten when families returned home from midnight mass on Christmas Eve. That meant it didn't start until around 2:00 am. Over the years it became a meal eaten in a restaurant at a more conventional dining time, and became much more accepted at any day leading up to Christmas."

"I see."

"We always eat ours at Antoine's. The food is to die for, dear."

"I can't wait. All these customs and traditions are fascinating."

"That bodes well for your future with my Laurent."

I smiled and leaned closer. "So, you approve, then?"

She gave me only a small smile in return. "You shall see."

When we arrived at Antoine's, we were shown to a spectacular private dining room. The long table was set with candles and sparkling crystal stemware. On each plate was a folded napkin and on top was a lovely crystal ornament engraved with our names, like a place card and tied with a red ribbon.

Lobo and I found our spots, and he pulled out the chair for me.

His grandmother was at the head of the table, Laurent was to her immediate left, and I was beside him. Including cousins and children, there were eighteen chairs.

Claude and Cecilia sat across from us. Delphin sat on my other side along with his partner, whom he introduced as Chad.

The night progressed with wine, good conversation, pleasant Christmas music playing low in the background, and a four-course meal that was amazing.

After dessert was served, Jacqueline tapped her butter knife against her wine glass.

"May I have your attention?"

The room, which had been filled with the muffled sounds of nine different simultaneous conversations, quieted.

"I wanted to welcome our Laurent's lovely Hope. I'm extremely pleased to have met her, and I hope the two of them will be making many more trips home. You're always welcome here, dear Hope. And with that in mind, I have a gift I'd like to bestow on Laurent's lady." She picked up her handbag and withdrew a dark blue velvet case.

"Laurent, dear, do you mind switching with Hope for a moment?"

He complied, standing and holding the chair out for me. Once I was seated next to her, Jacqueline patted my arm and slid the case across the tablecloth.

"I watched you and my grandson over the time you've been here. I've never seen a couple more suited for each other. You care deeply about each other. That much is evident from your body language." She patted my hand again. "Oh, don't be shy. The way that boy looks at you, it's obvious he's crazy about you. So." She paused. "I want you to have this."

She pushed the case toward me.

I glanced at Lobo, but he just shrugged.

I cracked it open and stared at a stunningly beautiful necklace made of a circlet of hundreds of diamonds. My eyes got huge, and I lifted them to Jacqueline. "You want *me* to have this?"

She nodded. "It's been in the family for generations. It's always been my intention to pass it to my oldest grandson's lady. Now that's you."

"But I couldn't—that is—I can't possibly… I mean… I can't accept something like this."

"I want you to have it. That's that. I would be thrilled if you wear it to the Christmas Ball Saturday night. Would you do that for me, dear?"

I looked at Lobo. This wasn't part of our arrangement. I wasn't supposed to be going home with a piece of his family's heirloom jewelry. But here, now, in front of everyone, he nodded. I'd have to return it to her before we left for Nevada. But for now, I turned and told her I'd like that very much.

I gazed around the table and caught Eve's eye. If looks could kill, I'd be dead. Like Delphin had told me, this would have gone to her if she and Lobo had married, if she'd stayed with him and waited for him to serve his time. But she couldn't do that. And this necklace would never belong to her now. The sight of it going to me drove her mad with jealousy, but I had nothing to do with that. As far as I was concerned, she only had herself to blame.

I closed the lid and squeezed Jacqueline's hand. "Thank you very much, and not just for this gift, for your kindness and acceptance. It means the world to me."

She smiled and cupped my cheek. "It's good to see it in the hands of someone who appreciates it."

Lobo's father sat across the table, draining his third gin and tonic. He snapped his fingers for the waiter, and Lobo tried to intervene.

"Perhaps you've had enough, father."

Claude's brow lifted. "You're going to lecture me about something? My son with no ambition? That's rich. What a disappointment your entire life has been."

My stomach knotted. I laid my hand on Lobo's knee and

squeezed. He covered my hand with his.

"Maybe we should go," I whispered.

Before he could respond, Rosalie started laughing. "You're a vile man, father. Always ready to believe the worst. Well, I've got something to tell you, something I should have told you years ago."

"Sit down, Rosalie," Lobo muttered.

"Let her talk, Laurent," Beau said. "She needs to do this."

Lobo sat forward, his elbows on the table, and folded his hands, dropping his head. I rubbed between his shoulder blades.

"It was me, Father. *Me*. That night. The accident. I was the one who borrowed your car."

"No. It was Laurent," he insisted, shaking his head at his daughter.

"What's this?" Cecilia asked. "What are you saying?"

"It was me, Mother. I hit that car. I killed the driver. Not Laurent. Me."

Claude shook his head. "No. No. It was your brother."

"It wasn't." Rosalie surged to her feet, pregnant belly and all. "It was me. He said it was him to protect me. He didn't want my future to be ruined, so he sacrificed himself for me." She pounded her chest, her voice getting emotional. "And I've had to live with the guilt of it all these years. I had to watch him go to prison for me. I had to watch you besmirch him, Father. Saying he was worthless, saying he was a disappointment. He wasn't. He was my protector. My big brother who would never let anything happen to me, even if it was my fault. Even now, he didn't want me to tell you the truth. He begged me not to." She looked from Laurent to her father and slammed her fist on the table. "I owe him my life. Everything I have is because of his sacrifice. And you... you owe him an apology."

Beau stood and wrapped an arm around his wife. "Let's go, honey. You need rest."

Before she let her husband lead her out, Rosalie turned and put her hands on Lobo's shoulders, then bent and kissed his head. "I love you, brother."

After they left, murmurs broke out around the table until Jacqueline banged her cane on the floor.

"Enough." Once the room quieted, she arched a brow at her son. "Well, Claude?"

He looked up at her. "Well, what?"

She motioned the curved handle of her cane toward Lobo. "Apologize to your son. If anyone on this God's green earth deserves one, it's him."

Instead, Claude grumbled something, stood, and stalked out.

Jacqueline let out a long-suffering sigh. "Well, I knew it. I always knew that story of yours stank to high-heaven. I knew you wouldn't have wrecked your father's car. You were too good a driver. Only thing I was wrong about was who you were protecting. I always thought it was more likely your brother. I'm sorry, Laurent. Sorry for everything. Sorry on behalf of our entire family. What was done to you was a terrible injustice. You deserved so much better."

"Stop, Grand-Mère. It's done. It's over. I told Rosalie there was no need for this."

"I'm glad she did what she did tonight. About time, I say."

I felt like Lobo had had about all he could take, and I leaned to his ear. "I don't feel well. I think I need some air. Will you walk me outside?"

"Of course." He pushed back his chair, jumping at the chance to escape.

"Thank you for a lovely evening, Jacqueline. And for this." I clutched the jewel box in my hand.

Lobo slipped it from my hands and passed it to his mother. "Could you see this gets home safely, Mother? We're going to take a walk and get some air."

"Of course." She stood and came around the table, wrapping him up in her arms. "I'm so sorry, son."

He rubbed her back, and they broke apart. Lobo took my hand, and we walked out.

"Laurent, wait!"

We turned in the doorway. Eve jogged over.

She slipped her hand on Lobo's arm. "Can we talk?"

He pulled her arm off him. "Not now, Eve. If you'll excuse us."

Her face fell, total disbelief lighting her eyes. She was furious, but Lobo didn't seem to care. He turned to me and led me out.

CHAPTER TWELVE

Lobo—

I led Hope a couple of blocks toward Jackson Square. We crossed the street, and I ordered us a café au lait from the takeout window at Café du Monde. Then we walked up on Washington Artillery Park and sat on the steps.

"The view up here is fantastic," she murmured, and sipped on her drink.

"It is."

"You want to talk about what just happened?"

"I did what I did. Like I said before, I wouldn't change it. What Rosalie did was unnecessary. I wish she hadn't brought it up."

"People needed to know, Lobo. It's not right the way they think less of you. You were her hero that day. Maybe the guilt of the price you had to pay has eaten her up. She needed to do that for you and for her."

"Guess so."

We sat quietly for a few minutes until she bumped shoulders with me. "Hey."

I turned my eyes to her as a light mist fell.

"Tell me about Eve."

I exhaled a long breath. Hope deserved to know what she was dealing with. "I hate to talk about her. I hate that I ever thought I loved her. She's not the woman I thought she was."

"Your grandmother said she dumped you after the accident."

"Yeah. The minute I wasn't the favored, untouchable son of the

Broussard family, she went after my cousin."

"What kind of woman does that?"

"A social climber. I'm glad I escaped a life with her. I feel sorry for Marcel. I wouldn't wish that bitch on my worst enemy."

"I think she has it in for me."

"You may be right. She dumped your cookies on the floor. I saw her coming out of the kitchen. You sure turned that around, though. Did you see her face when Gran praised you for offering to make more?"

"I did. If looks could kill, huh?"

"Don't worry. I've got your back. She can't hurt us."

"I'm not so sure about that."

"I am." I kissed her head. "Can I ask you something?"

"Of course."

"The candle you lit at the cathedral earlier… Who was that for?"

Hope cleared her throat and stared off in the distance. Her head turned away so I couldn't see her face.

"You okay?"

Her eyes shone with tears. "My parents."

"Your parents are deceased? I didn't know. What happened?"

She dashed the tears from her cheeks. "I was ten years old. We were in the car, and I was goofing off, throwing a rubber ball in the air. It got loose and bounced by my father's feet and rolled under the pedals. He tried to get it out and lost control. We drove off the road and hit a tree. I was the only one who survived."

"Oh, baby, I'm so sorry." I wrapped an arm around her and pulled her against me.

"I've blamed myself for their deaths."

"You were a kid. It was an accident, Hope. Don't carry that burden." I held her for a long moment as the mist covered our hair and coats with glittering droplets.

"I'm sorry." She wiped the last of her tears and took a breath. "I get emotional sometimes."

"That's totally understandable, baby." I rubbed my hand up and down the sleeve of her coat, a million questions popping into my head. "Who raised you after that?"

She huffed. "My uncle."

"Why do you say it like that?" My body went solid, tension tightening every muscle, and I'm sure she felt it.

"He had control of the insurance money that was left for me. He blew through all of it. Then he failed to make the mortgage payments on the house. It was repossessed."

"What an asshole."

"Oh, that's not the worst of it. When I turned eighteen, he opened credit cards in my name and ran up a ton of debt. He destroyed my credit. It's taken me years to recover. I still haven't paid it all off."

Fury surged through my body. I wanted to strangle this motherfucker with my bare hands. "What's your uncle's name?"

She frowned. "Kevin."

"Kevin Kowalski?"

"Yes."

"He still alive?"

"Sure is. Lives in Vegas. Why?"

"Just curious." I pulled her to her feet. "You ready to head home?"

"Yes, I'm starting to get wet."

Her hair was covered with sparkling mist. The corner of my mouth pulled up. "You look like a fairy covered in fairy dust."

She giggled. "I used to pretend I was queen of the fairies when I was a child. I'd dance around with fairy wings, a ringlet of flowers in my hair, and my magic wand. I'd turn all my stuffed animals into magic woodland creatures. Unicorns, mostly. They're the best."

I chuckled and laced our fingers together. "That they are. Come on, fairy queen. Let's go home."

We walked over to Canal Street and rode the streetcar up St. Charles. The driver was playing Christmas carols on his phone and the windows were fogged.

Hope drew a heart on the glass with the tip of her finger, then met my eyes.

I smiled. "When we stop. Remind me I've got something for you."

Her eyes lit up. "More surprises?"

"Just a little one." We listened to the driver sing along with Mariah Carey's *All I Want for Christmas Is You*. He belted it out, and we both exchanged a look, then started singing along.

When we stepped off at our stop, I laced my fingers with hers. In a few minutes, we were standing on the sidewalk in front of the big golden B on the gate of my grandmother's home.

Hope pulled me to a stop. "What's my surprise?"

I slipped my hand in my pocket and pulled out a strand of gold Mardi Gras beads, holding them up. I lifted my chin to the branches of the huge oak trees stretched above us like a canopy.

She grabbed them out of my hand, then flung them above us. They wrapped around a branch and caught, dangling like a decoration. She giggled, then her eyes got huge. "Will she be mad?"

I dropped a kiss to her lips. "I'll take the blame for you, darlin'."

She arched a brow and slugged me in the arm. "You don't take the blame for anyone ever again, mister."

"Oww. Yes, ma'am." I rubbed my arm and laughed. "Damn, the girl's got an arm on her. You play softball or something?"

"First base during high school."

"Thanks for the warning." I opened the gate and got my girl out of the cold.

CHAPTER THIRTEEN

Hope—

Lobo and I returned from grabbing a light lunch. We had a couple hours before the Christmas ball, but I didn't know how long my hair would take. So, I trooped upstairs to get ready.

I walked through the door, and my eyes immediately fell to the dress in a pool of wrinkles on the floor.

"Oh, no." I ran over to scoop it up, hoping someone here had a steamer.

My hands touched liquid, and a pungent smell, like in a nail salon, assailed my nose. "What the hell?"

A bottle of nail polish remover lay knocked over on the floor, and my once black dress now had streaks of faded brown where the remover had bleached its color away. I wanted to cry, remembering how much the dress had cost and how I'd scrimped to save for it.

I hung it on the door, determined to see if there was any way to salvage it. My eyes fell to the side seam. It was torn about two feet, threads hanging in loose tendrils that reminded me of Cinderella after her stepsisters shredded her dress. How did this happen? This looked like sabotage, and only one name came to mind.

I wasn't about to let that bitch stop me from going to the ball. I needed to call my very own fairy godmother to help me find a new dress.

I held the phone to my ear with my shoulder as I shoved my makeup into my cream-colored tote.

Delphin picked up on the fourth ring, as my panic was starting to rise.

"Hey, bestie."

"I have a problem."

"What is it?"

"I'm pretty sure Eve destroyed my dress. I don't want to tell Lobo—I mean Laurent, because I don't want to start any drama at the ball with his family."

"But aren't you his family now?"

I stayed silent, struck by his comment and unsure how to answer.

"We'll circle back to that. How bad is it?"

"It's torn and bleached."

"Damn, she's a bitch."

"No arguments from me on that one. Can you help me? I mean, you are always so put together, I figure you know the places to go."

"Oh, babe." I could practically hear him blushing through the phone. "You're so sweet. And of course, you're right. I'll be there in ten. Make it fifteen. I just noticed my eyebrows. I cannot be caught dead with these bushy things."

"Great! Thank you."

I immediately jammed the dress into my hanging bag and cleaned up the mess she made. I didn't want to risk Lobo seeing what happened.

Grabbing hair items and shoes, I shoved them into my tote with my makeup. Then I snatched the garment bag off the door and made my way downstairs.

"Where are you going?" Lobo called from the sitting room.

"Delphin is helping me get dolled up for the ball. I'll meet you there."

"You sure? I can wait on you." He rose from the couch and walked toward me.

"No, no." I glanced at my phone. "At this rate, I'm probably going to be a few minutes late, and I don't want you to be, too."

"All right, but wait a minute." He dashed up the stairs only to return a few minutes later, carrying the velvet box.

"Are you sure you want me to wear this?" My eyes searched his.

"Of course. Now go, I'll see you soon." He gave me a peck and then held the door for me as I carried my bags out.

Delphin pulled up just as I made my way down the steps.

"Hop in."

I threw the bags in the back and climbed into the passenger seat.

"What is that smell?" He wrinkled his nose.

"Sorry. I had to bring the dress. I didn't want Lobo to try to bring it to me, thinking I'd forgotten it."

"Did she dump the whole bottle?" He rolled the windows down and practically hung his head out.

"From the looks of it, I'm pretty sure she did."

"Well, that's going straight to the dumpster."

We drove past storefronts with window displays of dress mannequins posed and clad in the latest fashion. Delphin swung the car into an open spot in front of a small boutique with a window display full of sparkling gowns.

Yanking the door open, my eyes landed on a hanging sign with the word *closed* written in big black letters, and my heart sank.

"It's closed," I whined.

"Not for you." He waggled his now perfectly shaped eyebrows at me.

My head tilted to one side. "Huh?"

"This is my store," he proudly proclaimed.

"Yours?" My face lit up. "You, sir, are amazing."

He opened the door to a gentle tinkling of a bell tied to the knob with a pale blue ribbon.

The lights flipped on and rows and rows of colorful, gorgeous gowns filled my gaze.

"These dresses are something else."

"I mostly cater to the pageants and masquerades. Now, let's see, let's see." He thumbed through the racks, and pulled a lace and jewel covered white mermaid dress out. "What about this one?"

"I'm not wearing white. People will think I'm a bride."

He looked at the dress in his hands. "Yes, but it'd really piss off Eve."

"As tempting as that is, I'm not wearing white."

"Okay, okay," he conceded.

He tapped a finger to his lips, thinking. "I've got it. No need to look at any others."

I expected him to move to another aisle, but he went to a backroom. A few moments later, he walked out, carrying an incredibly large bag.

"This one came in last week, and it is to die for." He pulled me behind him to a dressing room. A white pedestal sat outside the door, waiting for a customer to show off their dress to friends or family.

He unzipped the bag and gold taffeta spilled out.

"Gold?"

"Yes! In a sea of black and red, you, my dear, will be a vision."

"All right, I'll try it on."

Delphin helped me step into the dress, pulling the bodice up.

It was a strapless gown. The bodice ruched at my breast, drawing the eye to my ample cleavage. It was a true ball gown, the skirt as big as any I'd ever seen. Surprisingly, it didn't weigh as much as I expected.

Delphin zipped it up, and I stepped onto the pedestal, studying my reflection in the mirrors that curved around me in a semicircle.

Delphin stood behind me, nodding like a schoolboy. "The necklace Grand-Mère gave you is going to look gorgeous. Let's try it on."

He walked over to the velvet box lying atop my bags and popped it open. The diamonds glimmered in the lights, causing prisms of rainbows to dance across the walls as he walked toward me.

He clasped the necklace, and I stared at the image reflected back.

"Gorgeous," he murmured.

My hand fluttered to the jewels, taking it all in. A circlet of three rows of diamonds encircled my neck. "It's not too much?"

"It is exactly the right amount. And Eve will be green with envy."

I stepped down, intent on grabbing my shoes, and realized a problem. "It's a bit long." That's all I need—to fall on my face.

Delphin bent on one knee, and folded the dress a bit. "Nothing a little hem can't fix."

He got his pins and began placing them.

"So, that was some dinner the other night," Delphin commented around a pin sticking out of his mouth.

"Yes."

"I can't believe Laurent went to prison for Rosalie." He shook his head.

"He's a good man, to a fault."

"Clearly. My brother would be shit out of luck. I'm not about to wear those raggedy prison uniforms. I mean, talk about no form."

"I'm sure the prison uniforms were the least of Lobo's concerns." I met Delphin's eyes in the mirror.

"Well, he has always had a bit grungier style."

"I can't believe his dad didn't apologize for being a complete dick to him all these years."

"I know." He squinted in the bright overhead lights. "I wouldn't expect him to, though. He's never been one to admit when he's wrong."

"Geez, you'd think restoring some kind of relationship with your son would be more important." I shook my head.

Delphin shrugged. "What can I say? The family's crazy."

"I suppose most families are dysfunctional in one way or another."

"Word. All right, pinning is done. Take it off, and I'll go do a quick hem while you get the rest of you ready."

"Thank you. You're a lifesaver."

"I am, aren't I?" He rolled his eyes and waved me to the dressing room.

After throwing on a shirt and jeans so as not to be standing in my bra and panties, I picked up my tote and carried it to the expanse of mirrors.

My curling iron heated while I brushed out my hair. I styled long loose curls and then weaved them into an Elsa style braid that hung over my shoulder.

Leaning forward to apply my makeup, a thought popped into my head.

"Delphin?" I called toward the back.

"Yes?"

"Do you have any pictures of your grandfather?"

"Sure, why?" He appeared in the doorway, carrying the dress.

"I've been trying to come up with a gift for Lobo. His grandfather meant the world to him. Lobo's been upset that he died thinking the worst of him. I thought maybe if I could get a photo of the man, I could blow it up and put it on canvas or have it framed or something."

"Well, in that case, I can do you one better. My mom always pulls the photo albums out around the holidays. I saw a shot of Laurent and him together in-front of Grandpa's plane."

"That's right. He told me about that on our way out here."

"Yeah, Grandpa used to take Laurent out in his Cessna all the time. Used to call him his co-pilot."

"Could you get a copy for me? That would be perfect."

"Of course, dear."

I slid into the dress, while Delphin carried his own tux bag to a dressing room.

I was finishing the last touches of my smokey eyes when his door swung open. He walked out in a midnight blue suede tux jacket with black pants and bow tie.

I raised a brow. "Fashionable as always."

"Thanks, girl. And you are stunning." He snapped his fingers back and forth. "Let's go shove it to Eve." He looked at his Rolex. "Should only be about ten minutes late."

I hooked my arm in his. "We sure know how to make an entrance."

"Laurent's mouth is going to hit the floor."

We arrived about twenty minutes later.

The venue was a tall renovated historic bank building on Baronne Street. The outside was lit with beams of purple lights for the charity that was to benefit from this annual ball. The entrance was gold art déco from the 1920s. Mahogany trim, marble columns, travertine floors and brass flourish, and the most amazing crystal chandeliers embellished the foyer.

Delphin and I stepped into a huge two-level ballroom with ornate columns supporting a second level gallery with arched overlooks. Two enormous chandeliers hung from the ornate, carved, coffered ceilings.

I stood at the top of the stairs, more nervous than I'd ever been. This wasn't a job anymore. Feelings were involved. I liked Lobo. More than liked him. I was falling in love with him. I wanted to wow him, yes, but I also wanted to make a good impression on his friends and family.

I knew everything Delphin had done for me was more than amazing, but a part of me was afraid it was too much, too over-the-top. I wanted his grandmother's approval. A lot seemed to be riding on it.

Suddenly I was trembling.

Delphin whispered in my ear. "There he is."

I followed the direction of his gaze and found him halfway across the ballroom, standing with his family.

A murmur ran through the crowd. His brother nudged him, and Lobo turned. When his eyes landed on me, he froze.

"That's the reaction I was going for," Delphin whispered. "That's the look of a man completely enthralled with you. Dare I say it's the look of a man in love?"

I wasn't so sure, but a girl could hope.

"See the look Eve is giving you?" He chuckled. "We knocked Laurent's socks off *and we pissed off Eve.* Two birds, one stone. Mission accomplished."

I watched Lobo approach. His eyes never left mine. I picked up my skirts and descended the steps. He waited for me with an arm extended. I slipped my hand on it.

"You're ravishing. Is this the dress you brought?" He frowned, his gaze sweeping over me.

"I had a last-minute spill. Your cousin was kind enough to find me a replacement."

"And on such short notice. I'll have to thank him. You're the most beautiful woman here tonight, Hope. Absolutely gorgeous. Come on. I want to show you off to Gran. Her necklace looks like it was made for this dress.

My hand went to my throat.

Jacqueline turned when we approached, and her eyes latched on the necklace. "Why, it looks made for you, my dear. That dress is absolutely perfect for it."

"Thank you. Delphin chose the dress."

She nodded. "He has an eye for these things. Come, my dear. I have some people I'd like to introduce you to."

I spent the next half hour meeting many of New Orleans' high society, including several politicians. Lobo, thank God, stayed right by my side with his hand at the small of my back.

The event photographer came around and took several photos.

A waiter with a tray of long-stemmed glasses came by and offered us white or red wine. I chose white, Lobo chose red.

He leaned toward my ear. "I promise I won't spill it on your lovely dress."

"It's only borrowed. I turn into a pumpkin at midnight."

"I doubt that." He laughed, then peered at the hem. "Show me your glass slippers."

I lifted the dress enough to show him my strappy gold sandals.

"Even better."

Eventually, Lobo made our excuses and dragged me to the dance floor. I was surprised to find he was a good dancer, whirling me around in a sea of other gowned women and their partners.

"You've come to these events before, I see."

"There were always a long line of Masquerade and Mardi Gras balls. I had to learn to dance at a young age. Like I said, Gran had big plans for me. I think she would have liked to see me in politics. That all changed when I confessed to manslaughter."

My face sobered at the mention. I felt terrible for what he'd gone through. I knew he wouldn't want to hear me say how sorry I was or to express any form of consolation. That wasn't Lobo. Still, I'm sure he could read it in my face.

He dipped his head and bumped his forehead to mine.

"Want to hear a joke?"

I knew he was trying to put a smile on my face, and I gave it to him. "Sure."

"What did Cinderella say when she got to the ball?"

I giggled. "Dare I ask?"

"Nothing. She gagged." He waggled his brows.

"Oh, you're horrible."

He pulled me close and whispered in my ear. "I'll let you prove me wrong later."

Someone tapped Lobo on his shoulder, and he turned to see his brother.

"Can I cut in?"

"No," Lobo said, turning away.

"Come on. Olivia's in the restroom, and Aunt Edna keeps trying to drag me on the dance floor. You've got to save me."

"I don't want to dance with Aunt Edna, either."

"Come on. Please."

"Fine. But just one dance." His eyes connected with mine. "I'll get us another drink. Don't believe anything my brother says. They're all lies."

He relinquished me to his brother, who drew me in his arms with a smile, and we whirled away.

"Sorry, but have you met Aunt Edna yet?"

"Is she the one with the orange hair?"

"Yes, and five o'clock shadow and the mole with the big hair growing out of it." He shuddered, and I giggled.

We whirled around and I noticed Eve approach Lobo, where he stood near the bar. He tried to ignore her and even walked off without getting waited on. I tried to follow him with my eyes, but lost sight of him in the crowd.

When the dance finished, I excused myself. "I really need to find the ladies' room."

"Of course." His brother bowed. "Thanks for saving me, Hope." Then he pointed me toward a hallway. "It's through there. If you run into my wife, tell her I'll be at the buffet."

"I will." I made my way toward the hall and noticed Lobo and Eve out on a small terrace. I picked up my skirt and got closer. The door had been left ajar an inch, and I could hear their voices. I was about to step outside and save Lobo from the vile woman when I heard what she was saying.

"Why in the world would you take the fall for your sister? How stupid. You threw your life away. You threw *us* away." She grabbed at his arm.

He shrugged her off. "You were the one who threw us away. After they arrested me, you dropped me like a rock. You were making a play for Marcel before the jury even returned a verdict."

"It doesn't matter. None of that matters now. Don't you see?" She pressed against his chest. "We can be together now. You can take your rightful place in New Orleans society. We can—"

His fists locked around her wrists and pulled her clinging hands off him. "Jesus Christ, Eve. You've got a husband. Have you forgotten him that easily?"

Lobo stalked a dozen feet away and lit a cigarette, but Eve followed him.

"I can get a divorce. We can be together. It should be me in your bed. It should be me wearing that necklace." She pointed toward the event space, tugging on his arm.

He shoved her away again. "Is that what this is about? You're jealous of Hope?"

"She means nothing to you. Say it."

"I won't. She's a thousand times the woman you are, Eve. It's taken me a long time to see the real you." His eyes roamed over her, his face a mask of disgust. "You may be pretty on the outside, but on the inside there's nothing but rot. Go back to your husband. I feel sorry for the bastard."

Her palm cracked against his face.

He flung the cigarette and took a step toward her, but she fled, tossing over her shoulder. "You'll be sorry for this, Lobo. I'll make you sorry."

"Get the fuck away from me, bitch."

I retreated around a tall Christmas tree into a dark corner. It wouldn't hide me if she glanced over, but she didn't. She stalked into the crowd.

I emerged from my hiding spot and watched her go, then heard the door opening and turned to find Lobo.

He ran a hand over his hair and dragged in a breath, the fury on his face was replaced by an unreadable mask.

I went to him, taking his hands.

"Your dance is over? I'm sorry. I went out to get some air and—"

"I heard what she said."

"I suppose that didn't look too good, me with my ex…"

"She wants you back. That much was clear. But I heard you set her straight."

"I don't want anything to do with her, Hope. That's ancient history for me. I have no interest in reliving it or trying to reshape it."

"I'm glad to hear it."

That got a smile out of him. "What do you say we sneak out of here? I'll call a car to pick us up. Hell, my grandmother probably has her limo on standby out there. I can have it take us home and send it back before she realizes it's gone."

"I'd love that."

We crossed paths with Delphin on our way to the entrance.

"Don't you two look the perfect couple? I really must get a photo." He whipped out his phone and positioned us in front of a fern. I pressed close to Lobo, and we smiled at each other, our secret rendezvous on our minds.

"Good?" Lobo asked, already grabbing my hand and starting to drag me away.

"Perfect." Delphin smiled at his phone, then looked up and frowned. "Where are you going? You're not leaving already, are you?"

I put the back of my hand to my mouth. "It's almost midnight. He's stealing me away."

Delphin winked. "Well, well. Cindy found her prince."

"Thanks for the dress."

"It's just a loaner, darling. Don't let him rip it off you."

"No promises," Lobo threw over his shoulder as I fast walked to keep up with him.

Coming out into the cool night air, Lobo shrugged out of his tux jacket and set it over my bare shoulders, then pulled me along to a long black limo parked at the curb, the driver leaning against it, playing on his phone.

"Is this Jacqueline Broussard's car?"

He looked up, straightening. "Yes, sir."

"I'm her grandson. She'd like you to run us to the house and then return."

He shoved his phone in his pocket and opened the rear door. "Yes, sir. Anything beats standing here."

I scooted in, and Lobo gathered my skirts, shoving them in the door.

"That's some dress, Miss," the driver commented. When we were both in the backseat, he closed the door, jogged around to the driver's side, and before we knew it, we were pulling away from the curb and riding through the streets toward the northeast.

CHAPTER FOURTEEN

Hope—

Lobo keyed the door to the Broussard home and tugged me toward the study.

"Let's have a drink." He slipped his jacket from my shoulders, pressing a kiss to my shoulder.

"That sounds fabulous. Let me just get out of this gown. I'll be right back." Our linked hands held, stretching out until he was forced to let my fingers slip from his.

"Don't be long, gorgeous."

I hurried to my room, and before I did anything else, I removed Jacqueline's necklace, setting it on the cherry wood dresser. Then I slipped off the gown and dressed in a pale champagne sequined mini dress I'd brought from Las Vegas, not knowing what type of events we might be attending. Now I thought it was perfect for what I had planned. I slipped on a matching pair of heels. My phone dinged, and I picked it up off the bed to find Delphin had texted the photo he'd taken of Lobo and me with the caption, *Perfection.*

I studied us. We looked good together, and we looked happy. I smiled and did a selfie in my little dress and sent it. It only took a moment for me to get an emoji back of a smiley face with its eyes popping out and its tongue hanging.

Delphin: Wowza. Have mercy on the poor boy.

I typed a reply.

Me: Gonna tell him I love him. Is this the right dress?

Delphin: Hell to the yes. You go, girl. Go get your man.

I laughed and returned to the study.

Lobo turned with two glasses in his hands, and his eyes swept over me.

He said nothing. Nothing.

I didn't smile. I didn't know what to do with that.

He was a tall, broad, sexy man in slacks that fit him like a glove and a few hours of stubble on his jaw. I'd never seen a man more attractive.

I'd thought about him for months, often regretting I hadn't left him my number. We were easy together. I didn't know how else to describe it. When I was with him, I was happy. But I knew he hated what I did, and I wasn't so sure about what he did, either. The MC seemed like family, but they were hardly boy scouts.

This was a big step I was taking—a big risk. I could easily end up with a broken heart. His silence had me second guessing everything.

Finally, he emitted a long, low whistle. "You take my breath, sugar. I think I like this one even better."

I flushed at his words. Hearing compliments from this man meant more than any of the others I'd ever received. I smiled broadly, relief washing over me as I came forward. "Thank you."

He passed me a glass and clinked his to it. "A toast to the belle of the ball tonight."

"And to the handsomest man there."

He huffed a laugh. "This isn't the real me. You know that, right?"

"I do, but you clean up nice." I ran my fingers down his studded tux shirt. "I, um… had an idea on the way over here."

"Oh, you did? And what is that?" He loosened his bow tie until it hung from his collar. Something about that was so sexy.

"I thought maybe we could make use of the carriage house again. You could build us a little fire, and I could bring the faux fur throw blanket from my room, and we could get cozy."

"I like the way you think, Miss Hill."

"Thank you, Mr. Broussard." I nodded to the wine he'd opened at the bar. "You should bring the bottle."

He grabbed it, taking my arm. "Let's make our escape before the rest of the crowd comes home."

***

Lobo—

Hope was stunning.

My dick thickened.

That little gold dress swung around her hips, and she was the walking definition of temptation with long smooth legs and an incredibly sexy ass.

I blew out a breath. Sex and love were fucking complicated enough without throwing in the parameters of this relationship that had started out the way it had.

We strolled across the courtyard to the carriage house and climbed up to the second level.

I bent and built a fire, then turned. Hope stood at the window, looking out at the starry night sky. She seemed nervous, which was crazy. We'd been together before, we'd been together *here* before, and this had been her suggestion.

She seemed sad… or perhaps lonely. I didn't want to think of her as lonely.

I wanted her to drop that dress and walk across the room to me. I wanted her hot and needy and wet.

My eyes swept over her legs. I dragged in a deep breath and shoved my hands in my pockets to keep from grabbing for her, pulling her close, and bending her over the end of the bed. She seemed distracted. "Are you okay, sugar?"

I moved behind her.

There was a foot between my cock and her luscious ass that I couldn't seem to keep my eyes off of.

Hope turned, her palms settling on my chest, and tipped her face up to mine. "Are you happy?"

Even with her in those gorgeous stilettos, I was tall enough to look down at her. My eyes traveled across her long neck to that glorious cleavage. My balls ached at the thought of getting her naked, running my hands over every curve, and fucking her hard and deep. What had she asked me?

"Am I happy?" I stroked the back of my finger along her upper arm. "At the moment I'm as happiest man on the planet. Why?"

Her gaze moved over my face, then locked on my mouth, and she licked her lips.

My cock pulsed, images of her on her knees and sucking it down filled my head.

"What are you thinking?" she asked.

"You don't want to know."

"I do."

"I was thinking of you, naked and on your knees for me."

The corners of her mouth tipped up. "I see."

"Do you? Around you, it seems, my cock stays hard all the time. Does that make you happy?"

Her eyes glittered. "It does."

"And?"

"A man like you can overwhelm a girl if she's not careful."

"Feel like being overwhelmed right now, Miss Hill?"

"Maybe we should talk first."

"Talk is overrated." I pulled her into my arms and kissed her. I'd waited all night to hold her like this, then when she'd walked into my grandfather's study in this sexy-as-hell dress, she'd pushed my control to the limits.

I peeled the straps of her dress off her shoulders and let it drop to the floor. As I suspected, she had nothing on underneath it. Just her gorgeous body in those gold stilettos.

"You look like a goddess, baby." I scooped her in my arms and carried her to the bed, setting her down gently. She lay there, watching me as I undid the cufflinks at my wrist, then worked the studs all the way down the shirt front, pulling the tails free.

"I like watching you strip for me," she murmured.

"I'll strip for you anytime you want, my beautiful angel."

"Am I your beautiful angel?"

"Damn straight." I took her foot in my hand and slipped off her shoe, tossing it aside, then I massaged her foot and stroked up her leg. I did the same with the other, then put a knee between her legs and moved over her, kissing my way up her thigh, bypassing her sweet pussy and continuing up her smooth belly to climb her breast and suck one taut nipple into my mouth. I left it red and glistening and moved on to the other.

She moaned and scraped her nails over my scalp.

I lifted and kissed her mouth, my tongue chasing hers. She cupped my face, and I stared in her eyes as I sank my dick into her pussy without warning. I couldn't help it; I was driven crazy with need.

She gasped in a breath.

I swallowed, watching her eyes flare. I didn't have a condom on.

We both realized that immediately.

"I need to pull out and get a condom," I whispered.

"No. Don't." She clutched me tight, wrapping her arms around me.

I searched her eyes. "You sure?"

She nodded. "I'm on the pill, and I want you with nothing between us."

I stroked in and out, loving the delicious feeling of being bare inside her. I wanted to savor every fantastic moment of it, but I was so ready to blow I knew this time I couldn't last long, so I pumped harder, rocking my body against hers, stroking over her clit with every thrust.

She moaned. "So good. You feel so good."

I dipped my head and sucked hard on her nipple and felt her flutter around my dick and a rush of wetness flood over me.

She pulled on my hair, and I lifted, capturing her eyes again. We stayed locked that way as I increased the pace until I was slick with sweat and our bodies were slapping together. I knew this probably wasn't going to get her there, so I slipped a hand between us and toyed with her clit. I wanted her right there with me.

I stroked over it again and again until she bucked against me, her breathing coming faster. When I knew she was almost there, I sucked hard on her nipple, and she clamped down on me and her head went back as she gasped out my name.

I released her nipple and watched the ecstasy wash over her face. A few more strokes, and I spilled my seed into her, my jaw tensing and my body rocking. Then I stilled, my chest heaving, and I watched her face. Her eyes opened and returned to mine, and the most serene smile formed across her face.

I couldn't help but return it, feeling a euphoria like none I'd ever felt. This felt right. I felt like I was right where I was supposed to be. Right where I was always meant to be.

"I love you, Lobo," she whispered.

***

Hope—

"I've wanted to tell you—"

Lobo covered my mouth in a kiss, cutting off my admission. He was such a good kisser; I lost myself in the moment. His hand stroked my bare arm, and he kissed me thoroughly, brushing the hair from my face.

"Lobo?" I stared into his eyes, his weight on me a comfort. It was a dangerous conversation. I knew my words might change everything, but I had to take the chance. If things weren't what they seemed, I need to know. "I… this isn't… that is… I'm not play acting. I hope you know that. I'm not pretending. I'm not sure I ever was with you. Since the moment I met you, I've felt like everything in my life shifted."

"What are you trying to say?" He frowned.

"I'm trying to say…" I drew in a deep breath, praying he felt the same. "I'm trying to say it's real. More real than anything I can ever remember. And I know that wasn't our deal. This was supposed to be no strings and—"

His hands slid into my hair and held me as he kissed me.

Lobo was kissing me like he loved me, like it was more than sex and desire between us.

I'd waited so long, denied myself too long. I needed this. I needed a man of my own, a love, a confidant, a partner on this journey called life.

I needed him.

The kiss went on until we had to break apart to gasp in a breath.

He pressed his forehead to mine. "Are you saying you're in love with me?"

I nodded, the words sticking in my throat. He hadn't said it back. Internally, I prepared myself to have my heart broken when he told me he didn't feel the same. I waited on pins and needles.

"I'm gonna lay my cards on the table, Hope. This all started in a bar in Vegas. Then you disappeared, and it was like a dream that vanished with the sun. Then you showed up on my doorstep. And it was like God had given me a second chance. I may be a stubborn ass sometimes, but I'm not that stubborn or stupid to throw that chance away. This isn't fake for me, either. This is as real as it gets. I never thought it was possible. Never thought I'd ever find someone who suited me so perfectly, who understood my life and was willing to take me on. Is that what you're saying?"

Again, I could only nod, but now tears were rolling from my eyes.

He brushed them with his thumbs. I steeled myself to be brave. "Why are you crying?"

"You haven't said it back."

He grinned. "Baby, I'm falling in love with you, too. No—not falling—I'm already there. I *am* in love with you. This whole weekend has knocked the wind out of me. Everything has happened so fast."

"I know. It's crazy, I suppose. Maybe we should slow it down. Maybe we should…"

"No. Absolutely not. I don't want to slow it down. Do you?"

"No, but I don't want you to feel like I expect anything you aren't ready to give."

"What do you want out of life, Hope?"

"What every person wants. A home, a family, a partner to build a life with. What do you want?"

"I want those things, too." He studied my eyes. "Don't give up on me, Hope. Don't give up on us. Things will work out. We'll get through this trip, and when we get back to Vegas and…" He broke off, and I suddenly knew what had just crossed his mind, and I knew what he was going to say before he said it. "I'm not normally a jealous man, Hope, but when I think of you with someone else, some *client*, my chest tightens. If we were together, it would have to be exclusive."

"Of course. Obviously, I can't do that any longer. I don't *want* to do that any longer. I'm going to call my appointments tomorrow and cancel them. All of them." I stroked his cheek. "It's my sole source of income. But I'm willing to give it up, to walk away from it, because that's how much I believe in you. That's how much I love you. I'm willing to take a chance on you. On us."

"You won't be sorry. I'll never make you sorry, baby." He stood. "This calls for a toast."

Fifteen minutes later, we were curled up in the bed, watching the fire and listening to it crackle as we sipped on wine. Lobo's arm was around me, and I felt like I was home, like he was my home. It felt right, so right.

"I have a confession to make," I said.

Lobo set his glass down. "Oh? What's that?"

"I know your family is important to you, but I can't pretend to like Eve anymore. She's the enemy, and I won't treat her like she's anything but."

"That's a wise decision."

"I wanted to rip her hair out earlier."

He shook his head. "Can you believe her? She'd throw her marriage away, tear apart her family. For what? Because she's jealous of a stupid necklace."

"I think it's everything that necklace represents to her. You were always the prize. Not your cousin."

"I feel sorry for him."

"Don't be. He was kind of a dick for doing that to you. Doesn't that break the bro code?"

"Pretty much."

"Your grandmother seemed pleased tonight. The event was a huge success."

"It was. It'll be in all the society pages. You'll probably be the talk of the town. You and that fabulous dress."

"I just wanted to please your grandmother."

"She was very pleased. I could tell."

"Do you think so?"

"Absolutely."

"Lobo?"

"Yeah?"

I stared at him, then my eyes dropped to his mouth. When he noticed, he took the glass from my hand and set it next to his, then cupped my face.

"You're beautiful, you know that?"

"I can't believe this is happening."

"It's happening, sugar. Believe it."

CHAPTER FIFTEEN

Lobo—

The scent of beignets cooking in the kitchen across the courtyard carried to the window I'd opened in the carriage house. Estelle was always up at sunrise, preparing the morning meal. It wasn't sunrise. It was almost nine. We'd slept in late after the ball, and so, I was guessing, had everyone else in the house.

I turned, rolling up my cuffs, having shoved the cuff links in my pocket. Hope sat with her back to the headboard, the sheet tucked around her breasts, tapping on her phone.

A few steps and I stood by the bed, watching her and seeing her text.

Hope: Mr. Black, I won't be able to make our date on New Year's Eve, and I'm no longer going to be available for any future dates. My escorting days are over as of today. You've been extremely sweet to me, and I will always appreciate our friendship.

It didn't take long for her phone to vibrate with a response.

Mr. Black: I am indeed sorry to hear that, my dear. I hope all is well with you and wish you only the best. If you ever need anything, you need only ask.

She sat there, biting her lower lip.

"You okay?" I stroked her head.

"I was wondering if I should block his number."

"Do you think he'll harass you?"

"No, it's not that. I don't want you to think I'll go back to this."

"I'm not asking you to do that, baby."

"I don't want you to have any doubts."

"I guess I'll have to trust you. That's what this is all about, right?"

"Right."

She began texting again.

"You gonna go through the whole list right now?"

"No time like the present. I want to get it over with."

"Anybody gives you any problems, I'll handle them," I offered with a wink.

She smiled and kept on typing. "Oh, I'm sure you would. I don't think that will be a problem, but if it is, I'll block their number and let you know."

"You do that." I bent and kissed her head. "This gonna take long?"

Her fingers paused, and her eyes lifted to mine. "A few minutes. You in a hurry?"

"There's a platter of beignets with my name on them across the courtyard. So, yeah." I grinned.

"Beignets? Why didn't you say so?" Her fingers moved faster, and I chuckled.

Fifteen minutes later, we slipped into our rooms and changed clothes, then went down to the dining room. We were the first arrivals. Breakfast was laid out on the buffet, and I passed a plate to Hope.

Estelle came in. "Oh, it's you. Thought it might be Miss Jacqueline. She sure is sleeping late this morning. Last night must have tuckered her out."

"She probably needs her rest. I'm sure she'll be in soon. The aroma of these beignets will draw her in."

"Suppose so. Can I get you anything else, Mr. Laurent?"

Hope sat at the table and took her first bite, then moaned around the mouthful. "Oh, my God. These are amazing, Estelle."

The woman beamed. "Why, thank you, Miss Hope. I got more in the kitchen fryin' up now. You enjoy all you want."

With that she retreated through the swinging door, and I poured a café au lait for Hope and carried it to her, setting down the cup and saucer before her, then got one for myself and sat next to her with my own plateful.

She'd already finished almost every bite.

I dragged a fingertip through the powdered sugar on my plate and tapped her nose with it. "Slow down, Sugar. You heard her, there's more."

"They're so good."

I chuckled. "I know. I was raised on the things. Ever tried King cake?"

"No. Does she have one of those?"

"It's usually for Mardi Gras, but they've been served around Christmas. Maybe I'll talk her into making you one for Christmas morning. Would you like that?"

"That would be fabulous. So, what's on the agenda today?" She licked her finger and pressed it to the plate, gathering up every crumb.

"Not much until Midnight Mass tonight. I was thinking of swinging by and visiting my grandfather's grave today. Would you like to go with me?"

"I'd love to."

"We'll head out after breakfast, then."

My father strolled down and stopped to pour himself a cup of coffee. His eyes strayed to the two of us.

"Hope. Laurent. Good morning."

"Good morning," we both murmured.

He sat in his usual place and stared at the lace cloth, his forearms resting on it, and his hands clenching and unclenching.

I waited quietly, chewing my food, my gaze on him.

Finally, his eyes lifted to me.

"I'm sorry, son. I've treated you horribly. I should have had more faith in you. I should have known you'd never wreck that car. And even if you had, I should have stood by you. I'm truly sorry. For all of it. It's unforgivable, the way I've been to you. Still, I ask for your forgiveness."

It took me a minute for it to sink in, to make sure I'd heard him correctly.

Then Hope rested a hand on my knee and lifted her chin toward my father.

I knew what she was trying to communicate to me, and she was right. I set my napkin on the table and stood, then moved to my father.

He looked up at me, seemingly as shocked as I felt. Then he, too, stood, and we embraced. The last time I'd hugged my father, I think I was twelve, so I took a second to soak it in.

Eventually, we pulled back and stared at each other. My father's eyes were glazed, and he just nodded, as if perhaps he was too choked up for words. I felt the same lump and patted his shoulder. Then cleared my throat.

"I, uh, was just talking with Hope about going to visit Grand-Père's grave this morning. Would you like to come along?"

He shook his head. "No, you go ahead. I was there yesterday. Had a long heart-to-heart with him." He smiled. "Did me good."

"It seems so."

He cupped my cheek with his palm. "I'm sorry I let things get so bad between us. I don't want that to happen again. I had a splintering with my own father before he died, and I realized I don't want that for us."

I covered his hand with my own and nodded.

Grand-Mère walked in, her cane in her hand, and paused when her eyes fell on the two of us. She stared a moment, then continued to her seat, muttering, "'Bout time."

I moved to pull her chair out for her. "Good morning, Grand-Mère. Did you sleep well?"

"Well enough. I should have been up hours ago."

"You must have been exhausted from last night," Hope said. "The ball was a phenomenal success."

"It always is, dear." She studied Hope while I fetched her a cup of coffee. "You made quite the entrance. Quite the entrance indeed."

I came to Hope's defense. "She looked lovely, didn't she, Grand-Mère? We have Delphin to thank for that amazing gown she wore."

"Yes, I heard. He was quite proud of how well you wore it, Hope."

"I was telling Hope how pleased you were with her last night, and your jewels looked lovely on her, didn't they?"

"Yes, yes, quite pleased, indeed. You looked lovely, dear. I'm sure your picture will be in the society pages this morning. Speaking of, has anyone gotten the paper in yet?"

"I'm afraid I haven't," my father said, sipping his coffee.

My mother came in, and Grand-Mère didn't miss an opportunity to rub it in.

"Did we wake you with our conversation, dear?"

"Grand-Mère was only five minutes ahead of you, Maman," I informed her as I pulled a chair out for her.

"Thank you, dear." She patted my cheek, and I kissed hers.

"So, what do you and Hope have planned today?" my grandmother asked.

"I thought I'd go by Grand-Père's grave."

"Take the flowers off the piano and put them in the stone holder." She tapped her cane. "Estelle!"

The woman hustled in from the kitchen, wiping her hands on her apron. "Yes, Miss Jacqueline?"

"Be a dear and wrap up the bouquet on the piano. Laurent is going to take it to my husband's grave for me."

"Yes, ma'am. Right away." She moved off to do my grandmother's bidding.

"Laurent, don't go disappearing tonight."

"On Christmas Eve? Of course not."

"We have Mass tonight. And we'll be gathering in the morning to exchange gifts, then Christmas dinner will be served."

"We'll be here, Grand-Mère. Are you ready to go?" I asked Hope.

She wiped her mouth with her napkin. "Whenever you are."

I stood and pulled her chair out, then laced our fingers together and kissed her. When I broke off, I saw my grandmother smiling at us. I winked at her and led Hope out.

Estelle caught us in the foyer and pressed the bouquet wrapped in wax paper into my hands.

"Thank you, Estelle."

"You're welcome, Mr. Laurent. Miss Hope."

"Are we catching a streetcar?" Hope asked as we walked hand-in-hand out to the sidewalk.

"Lafayette Cemetery is just a short walk, actually."

"This is nice."

"What is?"

"Holding hands."

I huffed out a laugh. "Yeah, it is."

"It was nice your father apologized, huh?"

My smile faded. "Yes. I didn't really expect that."

She squeezed my hand and bumped my shoulder. "It felt good, though, right?"

"Yeah, it did." I dragged in a deep breath, thinking about how I felt. "You know, I thought it didn't matter. After all these years, I thought forgiveness would never come. I guess I figured I'd gotten beyond needing it."

"But...?" she pressed.

"But I feel like a great weight has lifted off my shoulders. One I guess I hadn't realized I was carrying around all these years."

"I'm happy for you, honey. I'm glad you two have made an effort to heal the chasm between you." She studied my face. "I'm really glad you made this trip. Not just because it brought us together, but because it brought you healing. You needed it."

"I guess I did." I carried her hand to my mouth and kissed the back of it. "For what it's worth... I'm glad you're here with me."

"Me, too." She pressed against me, and I wrapped my arm around her.

We soon arrived and walked through the arched wrought-iron gates of Lafayette Cemetery. I led her down the aisle and turned left and then right through the raised tombs. It was funny how I could remember the exact spot when I hadn't been here in a decade.

"This is it." I stopped before a white marble tomb with an arched trim. The name Broussard was engraved on the top. I set the flowers in the stone holder that sat in the center of the ledge that wrapped around the bottom at about knee height.

The Broussard tomb, unlike so many others, was well kept. I kneeled and picked up a small straw hand broom my grandmother kept tucked to the side, and brushed the leaves and dirt away, cleaning the immediate area. Then I returned it and stood.

Hope clasped my hand and squeezed it. "He meant a lot to you, didn't he?"

I nodded. "I wished he'd known the truth about the accident before he died."

"Somehow, I think he knows."

I wrapped an arm around her, pulled her against my side, and kissed the top of her head. "I hope so."

Hope's phone rang, and she pulled it out of her purse. "I'm so sorry. I should have silenced it." She frowned at the screen. "It's Delphin." She put it on speaker. "Hello, Delphin. We're at the cemetery, visiting your grandfather's grave."

"Hey, Delphin," I added.

He sighed. "Now I feel guilty for not visiting myself. Way to show me up, cousin."

I leaned in. "Good morning, Delphin. What's up?"

"Meet me for a Bloody Mary at Pat O's."

"Sounds good. We'll catch the streetcar and be there in about twenty minutes."

"I'll be waiting."

Hope leaned forward. "Goodbye, Delphin."

"Ciao bella."

I shook my head and chuckled, then pressed two fingers to my lips and touched the tomb. "Merry Christmas, Grand-Père."

CHAPTER SIXTEEN

Lobo—

A half-hour later, we joined Delphin at an outdoor table.

He stood, taking both of Hope's hands in his, and kissed her cheek. "Radiant, as always."

We sat and ordered from the waiter who scurried over, then collected our menus and retreated.

"Well, you two certainly stole the show last night," Delphin said, then lifted the folded paper that lay on the table and passed it over. "Have you seen this? Page six."

Hope and I leaned our heads together and flipped it open.

She read the caption below our photo.

"The woman on the arm of Laurent Broussard, grandson of Jacqueline Broussard, made quite the entrance in a golden creation styled by none other than New Orleans' own very talented Delphin Broussard. And don't they make a dashing couple? Cinderella has arrived, and her name is Miss Hope Hill."

Her eyes got big, and she stared at me. "Is this good or bad?"

I chuckled. "The reporter knows a beautiful woman when he sees one. How can it be bad?"

"Your grandmother's charity. I never meant to steal the spotlight. This shouldn't be all about me. It should be about Jacqueline and the charity that benefits from all the work she put into the gala."

"You worry too much."

Delphin lifted his chin to the paper as our drinks arrived. "If you scan down in the article, they talk about the necklace, too."

Hope frowned. "They do?"

I pulled it from her and read it.

"It appears the famous Broussard diamond circlet has found a new home. Could this mean a wedding is in the offing? Perhaps spring nuptials are in the future. Stay tuned, readers. We'll keep you posted with all the gossip that's fit to print."

"Oh, my," Hope said.

"Pfft," Delphin replied. "They say that stuff every year about some debutante or other. They have to give the old crows something to talk about, otherwise they wouldn't read this stupid rag."

"Stupid rag? They called you very talented."

"They did, didn't they?" He lifted his chin and fanned his face. "They wouldn't be wrong."

Hope giggled and sipped her drink. "This is so good."

Delphin held his glass up. "A toast. To New Orleans' new 'it couple.' Cheers."

I chuckled and rolled my eyes but clinked my glass to his and Hope's. "To the town's very talented stylist, and to its newest Cinderella."

"Will you be at Midnight Mass tonight?" Hope asked my cousin.

He leaned in his chair and crossed his legs. "Miss Midnight Mass? I'd be shunned by the family. I'll be there with bells on."

"Not literally, right?" I asked.

He rolled his eyes and looked at Hope. "He's such a stick-in-the-mud. Seriously, darling, he's no fun at all. I don't know how you put up with him."

"Don't criticize the man I love," Hope defended, looping her arm through mine.

That had Delphin sitting up straighter. "Oh, that's right. You were going to tell him you loved him." He eyed me. "I take it that went well. You two look absolutely lovey-dovey this morning." His gaze flicked to Hope and back to me. "I'm guessing that scrap of sequins you called a dress did the trick, eh?"

I about spit my drink out. "How did you know about that?"

He pulled his phone out and tapped on photos, turning it to me.

I lifted a brow, studying it. "You and Ralph in bathrobes?"

"Oops. Wrong picture." He swiped to another. "She asked my opinion."

"I see."

"Oh, don't look at her like that. I'm her fairy godmother now. Of course, I had to approve."

"Good Lord."

"In fact, I need to steal her away for about an hour. You don't mind, do you?"

"She hasn't even finished her drink," I objected.

"So, she can get a go cup," he answered.

My eyes moved between them. "Just what are you two up to?"

"None of your business," he replied, snapping his fingers for the waiter, who hurried over with two go cups.

"So, I'm supposed to just hang out here for an hour?" I asked, watching him transfer their drinks.

"Oh, please. I'm sure you're no stranger to sitting alone in a bar, cousin."

He wasn't wrong, so I let it slide, but I pasted on a put-out expression and folded my arms. "Fine. But I won't promise I'll still be here when you come back."

Delphin pulled Hope to her feet. "Come on, darling. Don't believe a word he says. He'll be here. If only to make sure no other man hits on you when we return."

She waggled her fingers at me. "I'll be back soon. I promise."

I watched them scurry out, wondering what they could be off to do. I downed my drink, then ordered another. Ten minutes had passed when a shadow appeared at my shoulder, drawing my eyes.

"Hello, brother. Drowning your sorrows? You lose that hot chick already?"

Blood stared at me with humor in his face. His ol' lady, Cat, stood next to him.

"Guess so. Care to join me? Maybe I can steal yours?"

He laughed and pulled out a chair for her. "Fat chance, asshole. This one's mine."

"What brings you two out?" I asked.

"We started coming here the day of Christmas Eve several years ago. Now it's become tradition."

"Nice. I like traditions."

"I do, too," Cat responded. They ordered drinks from the waiter. Once the man left, Blood turned to me after glancing around. "Seriously, where's Hope?"

"She left with my cousin."

He quirked a brow. "You sayin' your cousin stole your woman?"

"Something like that."

"There is no way that happened," Cat objected.

"How do you know?" I asked.

"Because it was clear as day at the party the other night that she was crazy about you."

That made me smile. "Oh, yeah?"

"Yes."

Blood studied me. "Did you fuck that up?"

"No. Everything's fine. I think they went off to do some Christmas shopping or something."

"Ah. Right. So, you and her exchanging gifts? What'd you get her?" He took one look at my face and burst out laughing. "If you could see the deer-in-the-headlights look on your face. I take it you haven't gotten her anything. You dumb fuck."

"Shit. What am I going to get her?" I looked between the two of them.

"Depends. How serious are you?" Blood asked. The waiter returned with their drinks and slid them on the table.

"'Bout as serious as it gets, I guess."

"Jewelry," Cat suggested.

"I think she's gotten enough jewelry this trip."

"Oh, really?"

"Yeah, my grandmother gave her a priceless family heirloom."

"You'll think of something." Blood patted my shoulder.

I stared at the table.

Cat sipped her drink, then gave me a side look. "She told us she fell in love with riding. Said it was her first time."

"No shit? Is that right?" Blood asked.

I sipped my drink. "Yeah. I suppose so."

Cat lifted her brows. "Maybe she needs her own riding gear. I mean, if you think she'll be sticking around."

I snapped my fingers. "That's it."

"You're not giving her a property patch for Christmas morning, are you? There are procedures for that shit, bro."

"Not yet. Someday soon, though. I was thinking of something else." I pulled my phone out and started scrolling. "I wonder if they can deliver." I looked at my tablemates. "They probably can, right?"

Blood exchanged a look with Cat, and they both burst out laughing.

"Damn, I don't miss those days," Blood said.

Cat slugged his arm. "You loved those days. Admit it right now."

"Yes, ma'am. Best days of my life, baby." He grabbed her arm and dragged her onto his lap.

I looked up from my phone. "Please don't get us kicked out of here."

"I'll take that as a challenge," he said, and began to tickle his ol' lady until she shrieked and begged for mercy.

CHAPTER SEVENTEEN

Lobo—

Downing my drink, I glanced at my watch as I stood in the study with my father, brother, and brother-in-law. It was almost 11:00 pm, and if we didn't get moving soon, we'd have trouble finding a seat. The cathedral was always packed for Midnight Mass on Christmas Eve.

"Why do women always take forever to get ready?" my brother asked.

"I don't know, but it's usually worth the wait," Marcel replied.

I was beginning to find that out.

The whole family had gathered here so we could go together. There were enough of us; we'd probably take up an entire pew, maybe two.

The sound of the front door opening and closing carried to us, and a moment later, in walked Delphin dressed to the nines.

"Your favorite cousin has arrived. We can go now." He pulled off his white gloves and made straight for the bar. "I see my brother is exercising his only talent and manning the bar. Make me a scotch on the rocks, dear brother."

"Make it yourself, jerk," Marcel snapped.

"Well, now. Aren't you in a festive Christmas mood?" He moved around the bar and made his own drink, then nabbed the stool next to me, leaning in. "I'd be in an odious mood, too, if I was living with that bitchy wife of his."

I tried to hide my grin behind my glass. "Knock it off, cousin.

Tell him you're sorry."

"I don't like to lie on Christmas."

I downed my drink.

He tilted his head. "I know something you don't know."

"I bet you do."

"Oh, don't get mad. It's a happy surprise."

"It's not another gold mini dress, is it? I don't think my heart can take any more surprises like that."

"Liar, liar, pants on fire." His gaze dropped to my lap. "No pun intended."

"You look at my crotch again, I'll knock your lights out, cousin."

His shoulders slumped. "Why is everyone so on edge tonight? It's like walking on broken glass around here. I say what's on my mind, people. Get over yourselves."

"Don't be a prick on Christmas Eve, Delphin," Marcel snapped.

"All of you hush," my father spoke up. "You're like eighth graders, I swear."

The door opened, and the women swept in, all dressed in their Christmas finery.

Hope looked gorgeous in a sage green wrap dress with long full sleeves that cuffed at the wrist, and a deep V-neck. It was formfitting to the knee and showed off her figure in a tasteful way. She'd topped off the outfit with gold heels for a little holiday sparkle.

I stood and kissed her. "You look beautiful, baby."

"Thank you, and you look very handsome."

I leaned close and whispered in her ear. "To tell the truth, I can't wait to get back to my jeans and leather."

That brought a smile to her face.

"Let's go. The cars are waiting," my grandmother announced, slipping on a long white velvet cape.

We all moved toward the foyer.

Hope slipped her hand on my arm, and we started down the front steps behind the others.

Estelle waited to close and lock the door.

Eve waved us on. "I just need to use the restroom. We'll catch up."

I looked at Hope. She didn't seem any happier about Eve hanging back in the empty house than I was. Who knew what Eve could really be doing?

"Come along." My grandmother shooed us on.

We had no choice but to climb into the waiting car. I kept a hawk's eye on the door as we all sat waiting. I was about to make up some excuse and return to the house when Marcel and Eve emerged, and Estelle locked the door behind them.

Eve slid into the long limousine and gave me a smug smile.

She was up to something. I knew it, but I also had a feeling she was playing the long game, and we wouldn't find out what she was planning until she sprang it on us at the worst possible moment. Eve was like that. I really dodged a bullet ten years ago.

The car pulled away from the curb, and we rolled through the streets of the garden district. The decorations were pretty, but my eyes kept straying to Hope's legs. I longed to run my hands over them. I settled for resting my palm on her knee and giving it a squeeze.

Hope covered my hand with her own. I glanced up and caught Eve's eyes on them. When they flicked up to mine, pure fury burned in them.

"What's the matter, Eve?" I asked, putting her on the spot.

She folded her arms and stared out the window with a lift of her chin. I was about to turn away and dismiss her when I noticed that damn smile again.

It wasn't long before we arrived at St. Louis Cathedral and went inside. We occupied most of two rows of pews. Hope and I sat behind

Marcel and Eve. I wanted to keep my eyes on her.

Soon we lost ourselves in the Mass, and I tried to let it go.

***

Hope—

We arrived home late that night, and Lobo and I went upstairs to our rooms. He pulled me into his with a smile.

His hands landed on my waist, and he kissed me gently. "I have something I want to give you."

My heart warmed. "You mean a Christmas present?"

"Mmhmm." He pulled a box from under the bed. It was a large white box with a red bow. "I don't want to wait until tomorrow when everyone will be here. I want to give it to you when it's just the two of us."

I sat on the bed and pulled the ribbon free, then lifted the lid. My mouth fell open. Inside was a riding helmet and beneath that, a leather jacket, gloves, and riding glasses.

"You got all this for me?"

He shrugged. "You seemed to like riding on the back of the bike with me the other day. I figured when we got back to Vegas, we'd be doing a lot more riding together. You need to have your own stuff."

I scooted off the bed, vibrating with excitement, and slipped on the jacket. It fit perfectly.

"Try the helmet. I had to guess the size."

I did, and he buckled it under my chin. It was snug, as it should be. I put on the gloves and glasses, and with my hands on my hips, gave Lobo a huge grin. "How do I look?"

"Hot. My sexy biker chick, come here." He pulled me to him and kissed me.

"I have a gift for you, too. Let me go get it." I dashed into my room and came back with the wrapped gift and held it out to him. "Merry Christmas, sweetie."

He sat on the bed and unwrapped it, tossing the pretty paper on the floor and holding up the picture. Delphin and I had made a copy of the photo from his parents' house, and I'd gotten a beautiful silver frame for it.

He stared at the image of him and his grandfather standing in front of a red and white Cessna. "Oh, my God," he whispered. "How did you do this?"

"With a little help from Delphin."

"I haven't seen this picture in years. I'd forgotten my aunt had taken this photo." He stroked his fingers over the glass. "My grandfather loved that old plane. He used to take me up in it when the weather conditions were perfect, and I was off from school." He looked at me with glazed eyes. "Thank you for this. It means a lot."

"You're welcome. Thank you for my gift." I twirled in the jacket, then slipped it all off.

He stood and hugged me tight. "Best Christmas gift ever."

I laughed. "I just wanted to give you a gift that would mean something to you."

Setting aside our gifts, we stripped down, crawled under the covers, and snuggled close. Christmas music drifted from downstairs. I lifted my head from Lobo's shoulder and met his eyes, frowning.

He smiled. "Gran loves to play carols on Christmas eve. Does it bother you?"

"Not at all. I love it."

He stroked my back and pressed a kiss to the hair at my temple. "You doing all right?"

"I'm doing fine."

"You've been a real trooper through all these events my

grandmother has planned."

"My pleasure. I've enjoyed it."

"So, you accepted this job for the money Daytona offered. He never told me a price, but it had to make it worth your while. But what about your own family? Did you have anyone besides that uncle? A cousin or someone who you usually spent the holidays with?"

"No one. If there were, I was too young to remember them."

"I'm sorry."

I hugged his waist. "It's okay. This is the best Christmas ever. And I have you now, right? I'm really happy."

He kissed my forehead again. "Good. I plan to keep you that way. And yes, you've definitely got me now, sweetheart."

I moved over him and kissed his lips—soft little kisses I hoped would show him how much I felt for him. I could feel his muscles tightening and his body coming fully aroused under me, so I broke the kiss and slid down his body, intent on showing him just how much I desired him.

His hands moved to my head, his fingers threading through my hair, and he moaned so deeply I felt the rumble in his chest. I slid between his thighs and licked his erection from root to tip, then took him into my mouth.

"Damn, baby," he hissed, his fists tightening in my hair. "That feels so fucking good."

I smiled on the inside and continued happily to take my man to heaven and back.

CHAPTER EIGHTEEN

Hope—

I woke up to Lobo rolling on top of me.

"Wake up, baby. Santa's been here."

I giggled at his grinning face. "Santa already came, and he brought me awesome gifts."

"Santa came twice last night, angel, or did you forget?" Then he tickled me until I begged for mercy.

We showered together, and I took my time soaping his body. He stood in the spray, letting me do as I pleased, until he could no longer keep his hands off me. Then it was his turn to glide his soapy hands over my wet skin. We ended up with me facing the wall, my hands on the tile, my ass tilted and him taking me from behind, and it was glorious. I reveled in the way his hands clamped on my hips, his grip tight, controlling and possessive. I loved the way he started slow, enjoying every stroke. Looking over my shoulder, I saw him watching his dick slid in and out of my wet pussy, and I clamped down on him and heard him groan.

Releasing my hip with one hand, his arm came around my waist, and those long fingers found my clit. He played with it in long soft strokes, dragging the pads of his soapy fingers back and forth again and again until I was rocking with him, my hips bucking, and begging for more. He gave it to me. I balanced on the precipice. Sensing that, he reached up and pinched a nipple, and I flew over into bliss, rocketing like a rollercoaster to the bottom.

His speed built until he was pounding into me through my orgasm, and I loved it. When he came, he came hard, holding me tight, wrapping his arms around me and sucking on my neck. I knew I'd carry the mark for days, and I loved that, too.

"Best Christmas morning ever," he whispered in my ear. I spun, going into his waiting arms. We held each other close, and I felt a connection I knew was growing stronger every day. The kind of connection that could last a lifetime. It felt so right.

I cupped his face. "Merry Christmas, baby."

He kissed me. "Merry Christmas, angel."

We dried off, dressed, and went downstairs. The cousins and their children soon arrived, and gifts were exchanged and opened.

Lobo sat in a chair, and I curled at his feet on the rug, happily watching the controlled chaos as wrapping paper went everywhere. Lobo stroked my hair, and warmth spread through me at the simple touch. I was happier than I could remember ever being.

He kissed the top of my head. I tilted my face up to his, and he gave another kiss to my lips. We smiled at each other; no words necessary to communicate the joy we both felt.

When I dipped my head, my eyes connected with Eve's across the room. There was something there, something that reminded me of the classic high school mean girl who was about to give someone their comeuppance.

I knew she absolutely hated me, and the funny thing was, it had nothing to do with me. Any girl Lobo had brought home would have been her target.

Soon it was time for their big Christmas noontime meal, and we all gathered in the dining room. The table was set beautifully with elegant China and crystal. Candles were lit and wine was poured. Lobo's father stood to make a toast, welcoming us all and giving his wishes for a Merry Christmas and Happy New Year.

Lobo and I clinked glasses—elegant gold trimmed goblets I was terrified of breaking. We sipped the wine and stared into each other's eyes.

Delphin was on my left and it was nice to have an ally, especially when I looked across the table at Eve.

We ate the meal, and everyone chatted.

Dessert was served, and the children ran off to play outside in the courtyard with their new toys under the watchful eyes of Uncle Delphin.

Coffee was served, and the relaxed atmosphere was broken when Eve stood. I felt my stomach drop when she looked at me.

She scanned the table. "One of us is a fake." Her eyes landed on mine and remained steadfast, a sickening curl to her lips.

"What are you going on about, Eve?" Jacqueline looked at her, almost annoyed.

"Miss Hope Hill, your favorite grandchild's beloved, the one you bestowed your heirloom jewels to, is nothing more than a two-bit whore."

Gasps rang out around the table as I felt my face flush red. She'd found out. Normally, I'd steel my face and straighten my back to such insults, but Lobo mattered to me. This family mattered to me. But when she was finished dragging me through the dirt, they'd think little of me. I wouldn't be fit to sit at this table.

"Eve, watch your mouth," Lobo spat, his voice icy with warning.

"What? You know I'm right. After all, you hired her." Her gaze traveled around the table. "She's a paid escort."

The words fell like the thud of a door closing on the life I thought Lobo and I could have together. Gazes flicked to me, awaiting a denial that wouldn't come.

Rosalie decided to act as my champion instead. "Where did you come up with this nonsense?"

Eve pulled a stack of papers from her bag, scattering them across the table.

My eyes fell to the sheets. It was a printout of my webpage for clients. *Hope Hill, Las Vegas' most popular escort* scrawled across in bold print.

Rosalie scoffed, "I doubt there's only one Hope Hill. It's not the most unique name." She glanced at me apologetically. "No, offense."

I didn't respond. I could feel my heart pounding in my chest. Lobo was squeezing my leg, trying to keep me grounded. If not for his hand, I would have already fled from the table and the judgment that would fill their eyes once they realized it was the truth.

"I thought that, too." Eve smirked. "So I found proof."

"Eve, enough." Lobo spoke sternly, but I could hear the layer of pleading buried under the bravado.

She reached into her bag again, this time pulling out my planner.

My heart sank to the pit of my stomach.

"It's all in here. All her appointments. All the men who hire her. All the men she probably sleeps with for money."

Lobo stood so fast his chair crashed to the floor behind him. "Stop it."

"This is outrageous." Jacqueline stomped her cane on the floor, trying to regain control of the situation. "I won't have such ridiculous talk. Sit down, Eve."

"You don't believe me." She spoke to the silent table. "See for yourselves." She slid the planner across the table to Claude.

He opened my planner and thumbed through it.

"Father, give that to me," Lobo snapped. "It's none of your business."

"My God," Claude murmured, staring at the pages. "It's true, Mère. It's all right here. Dates, names, amounts." His eyes lifted to mine. "You must be good at your job. Had my mother eating right out of your palm. Nice little bonus getting the jewels, huh?"

I stood on shaky legs. My eyes flicked to Rosalie searching for one ally, but even she, in her attempt to stand behind her brother, couldn't wipe the look of disgust from her face fast enough.

I turned to Jacqueline. I couldn't read her expression, but she stared at me, silent for once. I unclasped the necklace she'd given me from around my neck and set it on the table.

Lobo reached for my hand, but I pulled away.

"I'm sorry for misleading all of you. Yes, Laurent hired me as a rouse. We pretended to be in a relationship, trying to fool you." I turned to Jacqueline. "But it wasn't out of cruelty. He wanted you to be happy, to see him building a family. He didn't want to see your disappointment when he came alone, but he also wanted to spend the holidays together." I glanced at Lobo watching his Adam's apple bob as I spilled the truth to their scrutiny. "We met a long time ago… before he hired me. There's always been a spark between us. I tried to treat this as a job, but my heart wouldn't have it. I love him. This hasn't been fake."

Eve laughed, a wretched sound. "Well, if you believe that." She sneered at Lobo. "Then she fooled you, too. She probably does that to all her men, and believe me, it's many. She throws herself at you, makes you think she wants you to screw her and then"—she paused, turning her scorn on me—"sends you a bill."

"That's not true, and I'm not a whore. I don't sleep with any of my customers."

"But you slept with Laurent, so another lie falls from your mouth."

"I'm not lying. What I feel is real." I flicked my attention to Claude. "And I didn't want this necklace. I'd never keep something so precious." I slid the necklace forward.

I searched the faces around the table, but I was only met with looks of revulsion and distrust, so I ran. I refused to let them see my tears.

"Wait, Hope!" Lobo called after me.

Out of the corner of my eye, I saw his mother grab his arm as he shoved around the table.

"Laurent, let her go."

A commotion broke out, everyone talking and shouting at once. His father jumped to his feet, yelling at Lobo as I dashed up the stairs.

I ran to my room, pulled my phone out with shaking hands, and ordered a ride. Then I hurriedly shoved my belongings into my suitcase, probably forgetting some things in the bathroom, but I didn't care. I had to get out of here now. I had to escape it all. I couldn't deal with my life being outed in front of everyone or their reproach.

Maybe it wasn't fair to Lobo, but I couldn't do this right now. I couldn't hash everything out in front of everyone.

CHAPTER NINETEEN

Hope—

I dashed down the stairs and out the door. I was at the gate before I heard Lobo behind me.

"Liar." The words hit me like a whip.

I swung around to face him. "What did you just say?"

"You said you loved me. Was it a lie? Was everything between us all a lie?"

My face crumpled. "You believe her." The words came out in a shriek as I flung my arm in the direction of the house. "You believe Eve. That I faked this. That I'm going to send you some kind of bill." I spat the words, feeling like venom coming from my mouth.

"Why are you running?"

"She turned them all against me. Game over."

"They don't change anything with us." He gestured his hand back and forth between us.

"They change everything." I spoke the words he needed to hear—the truth. "I grew up without a family. I'm not about to take from you the one you just got back."

"That would be their choice to make." He invaded my space until he blocked out the sun. I caught the scent of his exquisite cologne. I'd never encountered a man who smelled as good as this man. My head told my body to shut up. "I don't give a damn about what anyone thinks."

"You do. They're your family. Of course, you care. It's the reason you came home."

He ran a frustrated hand through his hair. "Goddamn it, Hope."

"I'm not going to drive that stake between you and your family. You tell me it's their choice, and you may not feel it at first, but you'd come to resent me. I'd see that saddened look every holiday you spent without them. I won't do that." My shoulders slumped in defeat.

He couldn't argue. We both knew that.

The door opened behind him, and his father stood there. "Laurent. It's your Grand-Mère. She's had another episode."

He twisted to look back, but stayed where he was. "Where?"

"Marcel and Julian carried her to her bed. She's calling for you."

Lobo turned to me, his jaw working. He lingered, unwilling to walk away. He didn't want to let me go. Not like this. He extended his hand. "Come with me."

He didn't grab me and pull me along, he just held his hand out, giving me the choice.

Tears filled my eyes. I shook my head.

His hand slowly dropped.

The only man I wanted was standing in front of me, asking me to trust him.

He shoved his hands in his pockets, tension vibrating off him.

His jaw flexed, and his eyes glittered with frustration… or some other emotion. Pain, perhaps? But he didn't say anything more.

My heart shattered into a million pieces. He was a part of me now, and that space he left would never be filled. I knew that as surely as I knew my name. He was the love of my life, and I'd never find another one. But I couldn't make his family trust me. Why would they? My whole purpose was to deceive them.

"Go to her," I whispered. "I hope she's okay."

It felt like a giant chasm was opening between us. One I'd never be able to transcend.

"Laurent! Hurry!" his father snapped, looking at me like I was dirt under his shoe.

Lobo turned and jogged up the steps, slamming into his father's shoulder as he passed him. I had a feeling it wasn't an accident.

I watched him disappear inside.

The door closed.

I turned, feeling a crushing pain like none I'd ever felt before.

He was a client.

I was his escort.

I had no business thinking this could ever be more.

Eve had made sure of that.

The driver tapped his horn. I picked up my bag and climbed inside, leaving a piece of me behind.

CHAPTER TWENTY

Lobo—

I pushed through the crowd and sat on the bed next to my grandmother, taking her hand in mine.

"Please leave us," she said in a weak voice. "I want to talk with Laurent alone."

Looking over my shoulder, I hit them all with a look that cleared the room. When the door closed, she squeezed my hand.

"She's a good person, Grand-Mère. She didn't deserve that."

"Eve is a bitch. Always has been. Is it true what she said?"

"Hope was an escort. But we've fallen in love. She was giving all that up, and we were going to have a life together, and if you or the rest of this family didn't approve, I didn't give a damn."

"You're talking in the past tense. Why?"

"She just left. She was crushed. She knew she'd never be accepted by the family."

"I'm sorry, Laurent. Truly. Eve will spread the tale all over town. Nothing can stop that."

"Hope doesn't deserve to be dragged through the mud, especially not by that vile bitch."

"True." She patted my hand, her breathing labored.

"If you make me choose between her and this family, I'm going to choose her every time, Grand-Mère. I love you, but that's the truth of it."

"I respect that. And whether you believe it or not, I want you to be happy, my dear boy." She coughed.

"Are you okay?"

"I took a pill. I'll be fine soon."

"Did they call anyone?"

"My doctor's on his way." She squeezed my hand. "Don't worry about me."

"Of course, I worry about you."

"Dr. Ravens will be here soon, and we need to talk before he arrives. We haven't much time."

"Grand-Mère—"

"Is she the one? Truly the one?"

"Yes."

"And you love her?"

I nodded. "More than life."

"Then go after her. A love like that only comes along once in a lifetime, Laurent." She reached toward the nightstand. "Open that drawer."

I did as she asked.

"The red velvet box. Give it to me."

I handed it to her, and her shaking hands opened it. She dug inside and held out a ring.

"Give her this. It was my engagement ring and my mother's before that, passed down for generations. Maybe it will bring you luck. It's worth a fortune. If this doesn't impress her, nothing will." She smiled, a twinkle in her eyes.

"I can't take that."

"It's sat in a drawer for all these years, waiting for this moment. I always intended for it to go to you to give to your bride. I'm glad I held it when you proposed to Eve. I always knew she would show her true colors, and she did. But enough about that dreadful woman. Hurry. Go after Hope. Win her back."

I closed my hand around it. "You're sure?"

"I'm sure, if you're sure." She patted my cheek. "Love is always worth it, Laurent. Any trouble, any compromise, any sacrifice. You deserve happiness. Go get it."

"Grand-Mère—"

"We're a crazy bunch she'll be marrying into, but as long as the two of you have each other, nobody else matters, me included. Go. Hurry. And throw that conniving little Eve out of my house on your way out. Will you do that for me?"

There was a tap at the door, and it opened. Her doctor entered with his bag. I kissed my grandmother, stood, and moved out of the way.

"So, you had another episode, Jacqueline? Have you been taking your medication?"

"I may have forgotten with all the excitement this morning."

"And have you been staying hydrated, like I told you?"

She looked past him to me. "He nags me so. Dr. Ravens, this is my grandson, Laurent. He was just leaving, but he won't go until you tell him I'm fine."

The doctor turned to me with a pat on my arm. "She'll be fine, Laurent. Nothing to worry about."

"You're sure?"

"She just gets dehydrated, and her blood pressure drops without her medication. She probably got lightheaded. I'll take good care of her."

I blew her a kiss and mouthed I love you.

She winked at me. "Don't you dare come back alone."

I rushed out of the room and smack into Delphin.

"What's going on? Where's Hope? Is Grand-Mère all right?"

I grabbed his upper arms. "She's fine. I need your help. I'll explain everything on the way to the airport."

"Airport?"

"You're not going after that bitch, are you?" Eve stood with her hands on her hips.

I looked past her to her husband. It was time he manned up.

Marcel's jaw tightened. "It's gone far enough, Eve. You did your damage."

Her head whipped around, and her eyes narrowed on him. "Don't you tell me what to do."

I grabbed Eve's arm and spun her in the direction of the front door. "Get out of Grand-Mère's house. She told me herself to throw you out. You are no longer welcome here, you fucking toxic bitch."

Her mouth fell open, and she jerked her arm free. "I will not."

"You will, or I'll haul you out."

She whirled on Marcel. "Are you going to stand there and let him manhandle me? Do something."

Marcel shook his head. "Not a chance. It's over, Eve. We're over. I'm done. I'm filing for divorce tomorrow."

Her chin shot in the air. "I'll take everything. You'll have nothing." She spun and pinned Delphin with her venomous look. "Get out of my way."

Delphin bowed and held his arm out toward the entryway. "Be my guest, you bitch."

She grabbed her handbag and stomped out the door. "To hell with all of you."

After the door slammed, I patted Marcel's shoulder. "You know a good lawyer?"

"I do," Delphin offered. "It's about time you came to your senses, brother."

"Yeah, well, better late than never." He looked at me. "I'm sorry I didn't stop Eve earlier. I like Hope. I'm sorry she left."

"I'm going after her." I glanced at my watch. It had been almost an hour since she'd left. "We've got to hurry."

I pulled my phone out and tapped out a text to her.

ME: Did you go to the airport? Please don't leave, baby.
HOPE: Too late. I'm already here.
ME: Don't get on a plane, Hope, please.
HOPE: Already in the boarding line. I'm sorry, Lobo. For
everything.

My shoulders slumped, and I literally staggered back to drop into a chair.

Delphin pointed a finger at me. "Don't you dare give up that easily. Let's go." He held up his keys.

"She's already at the airport. We won't make it in time."

"Then you'll go after her." He lifted a brow. "Or aren't you the man I thought you were?"

"You're right. I've got to try. Let's go." I stood, and we both jogged to his car out on the street. On the way to the airport, I showed him the ring our grandmother had given me.

"Dear God. Why have I never seen this before? It's gorgeous. Hope is going to flip." He grabbed my arm. "But you have to make it special. You have to do this big."

"How?"

"We'll think of something."

Twenty minutes later, he was dropping me at the curb.

"Don't forget what I told you!"

"I won't. Thanks, Delphin." I dashed inside and looked at the departure screen. I didn't see any direct flights to Las Vegas. There was only one flight that departed in the last half hour, and that one left for Dallas. Maybe she was catching a connecting flight.

I rushed to the ticket agent for that airline. "My girlfriend just left on flight 1225 to Dallas. She's going to Las Vegas. What connecting flight would she take?"

The woman typed on her keyboard. "Let's see. That flight left at 4:22 and arrives in Dallas at 6:10 pm. There's a flight out on our airlines at 6:50 pm so she'd have a forty-minute layover, and she'd arrive in Las Vegas at 7:43 pm."

"What flight number is that?"

"Flight 884, sir."

"Can you get me to Vegas before flight 884 lands? I want to meet her plane at the gate."

She did some more tapping. "We do have a flight that leaves in fifteen minutes, but all I have available is one first-class ticket. It's twelve-hundred dollars."

"I'll take it."

"Yes, sir, but you'll have to hurry, and there won't be time to check any baggage."

I yanked out my credit card and ID. "That's fine. I don't have any."

She swiftly typed on her keyboard and got me booked.

"Hey, could you help me out with something?" I pulled the ring from my pocket.

"It's beautiful, sir. How can I help?"

"I need a stack of paper and a marker."

Her head pulled to the side, and she gave me a strange look. "Paper and a marker?"

"Yes."

She printed out my ticket and dug around under her counter and came up with the copy paper and a Sharpie, passing them to me.

"Good luck, Mr. Broussard. I hope she says yes."

"Me, too. Thanks."

"I'll call the gate and tell them you're coming. Hurry."

"You're a Godsend." I blew her a kiss and dashed toward the security checkpoint. Thankfully, the line was short. When I got through, I grabbed my shoes in my hand and ran all the way to gate seven. When I got there, an agent stood at the door, waving me toward her.

"Mr. Broussard?"

I came to a skidding halt and handed her my ticket. "Yes, ma'am."

"I hear you're trying to beat your girlfriend to Las Vegas to meet her plane so you can propose."

"That's right."

She scribbled something on my ticket, tore a piece off, and handed me a boarding pass. "Good luck, sir."

CHAPTER TWENTY-ONE

Hope—

I cried the entire flight to Dallas. By the time I boarded my second flight, I was exhausted, and doubt flooded my thoughts. What had I done? Should I have given Lobo a chance to convince his family? Had I made a huge mistake? He'd begged me not to leave, not to get on the plane, and I'd done it, anyway. What must he think of me now?

It was only an hour flight, and there was no one else in my row. Somehow, I was able to push the worries from my head long enough to doze off.

The ding of the pilot clicking the intercom on roused me as he announced our descent into Las Vegas. The Strip appeared out my window, and a minute later, we touched down. The plane taxied to the gate and when the pilot flipped the seat belt sign off, I stood and grabbed my bag from the overhead compartment. Filing slowly down the aisle, I thought about how this trip had started, how Lobo and I had joked about the story we'd made up of how we'd met.

When I'd boarded that plane, I'd had no idea how this trip would end.

The flight attendant thanked me for flying with their airline, and I stepped through the hatch into the jetway and down the long tunnel toward the gate.

There was a backlog at the exit, and I was at the end. When I finally made it through, I saw people lined up on either side of us as we exited. Every one of them held a white piece of paper and written on each one was the same thing in bold black magic marker.

JUST SAY YES

I walked through the line, and it curved around to the side. As I got to the end, there was Lobo.

I frowned. "How did you get here?"

"I had a little help from a ticket agent."

"How long have you been here?"

"About an hour. Look, I know you think you're doing the honorable thing by removing yourself from the equation and not making me choose between you or a relationship with my family. But I'm man enough to make that choice, if it comes down to that. I wasn't lying to you when I told you I love you. I don't want to just see how this goes. I *know* how this goes. You're the one for me. You're the one I want to have kids with, to fight over the tv remote with, to grow old with."

"You want kids?"

"Yeah, don't you?"

"I do. But what about your family? I don't want you to lose them again."

"Gran and I had a long talk. I explained what happened from the beginning and how if she made me make that choice, I'd choose you every time. She wants what's best for me."

"Even with all my baggage?"

"You're the best thing that's ever happened to me. I want to spend every waking moment with you, building a life with you. Will you marry me and say screw it to anyone who gets in our way?" He pulled out a gorgeous ring.

I stared at it, stunned, then looked around at all the people still standing there with their signs. "But... how is your grandmother? And where did you get this ring?"

"Gran's doing fine. Just dehydration. The doctor was with her when I left. She's the one who gave me this ring. She told me if I loved you, I needed to go after you and give you this. Told me to tell you, we're a crazy bunch you'll be marrying into, but as long as we had each other, nobody else mattered, her included."

My mouth dropped open. "She said that?"

"This was her wedding ring. Handed down for generations. She hoped it would bring us luck." I looked at the emerald-cut diamond surrounded by a design of pave stones.

It took my breath. It was the prettiest thing I'd ever seen. "I can't take her ring, Lobo. It means too much to her."

"She said she always wanted my wife to have it. Said I was always her favorite, and I'd had a bum deal. She said I deserve to be happy, and that means winning you back. She said if this didn't do the trick, I was out of luck."

"What about Eve and the way your father looked at me?

He chuckled. "Gran had me throw her ass out. Guess what else? Marcel is divorcing her. About time he wised up. And my father will get over it. He liked you. He'll come around."

"Are you sure about that?"

"The past doesn't matter, baby. We both need to let ours go. Life's not always fair, but we've got to move on and concentrate on the future." He dropped to one knee. "I love you. I can't live my life without you. So, how 'bout it, Hope? You gonna marry me or not?"

"Just say yes!" the crowd yelled out in happy unison.

I nodded, and he slipped the ring on my finger, then stood and took me in his arms as the crowded airport cheered.

"When did you plan all this?" I whispered in his ear.

"I may have had some help from Delphin. He made me promise to do it big. Is this big enough?"

I peeked at the crowd around us clapping and nodded, then I

clung to him tighter.

"I swear I'll work my butt off to give you everything you want," Lobo whispered.

"I don't want much. Just a home, and a family, and maybe a kitchen big enough to start a cookie business."

"From home?"

I nodded.

"I may not be loaded, but I think we can do better than that."

"I'm so happy right now, Laurent Broussard."

He pulled back as the crowd dispersed. "Good. Aim to keep you that way. Let's go. The boys are waiting downstairs in baggage. They weren't allowed through security without a ticket."

I grimaced at my rumpled travel outfit. "I must look a mess."

He chuckled.

"What?"

"You. Worried about being presentable for a bunch of t-shirt wearing bikers." He looped his arm around my neck and turned me to the escalator. "Come on. Let's go meet the family."

I grinned, tucked against his chest, and smiled. And I went to meet his other family.

EPILOGUE

Lobo—

As we walked out of the airport, the ol' ladies surrounded Hope.

I hooked an arm around my VP. "You get that information for me?"

Trick nodded. "Dude lives in a twenty-million-dollar estate up on Summit Club Drive. Runs a couple of pawn shops and trades in native American artifacts. That's where the real money comes from. Heard he rides around with a briefcase full of money. The dude's got a trophy wife who left him for another man about six months ago. Wife is claiming abuse. I got a hold of some police reports. Beat the fuck out of her more than once. How the hell he isn't doing time for it is beyond me. I figure if the dude disappeared, no one would mourn him."

We stopped by the bikes, and my eyes hit the mountains on the horizon. "Good to know. He destroyed my girl's life. He does not get to walk around scot-free."

"I'm with you. We watch his movements and make a move."

"He stole her inheritance. About two hundred grand in life insurance, plus he let the house go into foreclosure. Add that all up, I figure he owes her at least half a mil."

"Looks like he's going to have to leave it all to her in his will. We can have the club's attorney notarize any paperwork after he signs the fuckers. And if that's with a gun to his head, so be it."

We both chuckled, and I seconded his thought. "So be it."

"Gotta clear it with Daytona first, but after what he did to the man who hurt Cherry, I don't see him having a problem with this."

"Good to know."

Trick lifted his chin toward Hope. "So, you and Hope Hill, huh? Who'd have thought it?"

I grinned. "She's givin' that life up, brother."

"She might want to change her name."

"How does Hope Broussard sound?"

He cocked a brow. "You don't waste time, do ya?"

"Nope."

He slugged my arm. "Merry Christmas, Lobo."

"Merry Christmas, Trick." I craned my neck. "Where's Daytona? I need to thank him."

"He's over there kissin' on his woman. You might want to wait on that."

"You're right."

"Good to have you home, brother. Cherry brought her car for you two. Said she'd ride home with Daytona." He tossed me the keys.

I caught them in mid-air. "Thanks."

Trick glanced at the women. "Looks like she's fitting right in. Imagine that."

I watched her showing off her ring to the girls. "Yeah. Imagine that."

I could never have invented an ending like this holiday trip home ended. Not in a million years.

"Good Christmas, huh, brother?" he asked.

"Best Christmas ever, VP." Then I went to collect my girl and take her home.

Want to know what happens next?
*Get a **bonus epilogue**. In it the boys take care of Hope's low-down uncle and there's a wedding in the quarter!*

Want to catch up with the Evil Dead MC's Nevada Chapter?
You can read Daytona's story here in **CHARLOTTE: Soul Sisters book one**
You can read Trick's story here in **TRICK: An Evil Dead MC Story book fifteen**

Start my new spin-off…*Sins of the Father, The Evil Dead MC – Second Generation*
Book one:
MARCUS: Sins of the Father

Book two:
BILLY: Sins of the Father

And many more *Sins of the Father* books are in the works!
Please check out **my website**. On it you can find all my books as well as sign up for my newsletter.

Made in the USA
Monee, IL
02 October 2023

43867640R00111